HAVEN

HAVEN

REVENGE OF THE VIPER

D.C. AKERS

Acknowledgements

No one walks alone on the journey of life; therefore, I would like to thank those who joined me, and walked beside me, and helped me along the way continually urging me to write.

Perhaps somehow this book and its pages will be seen as "thanks" to all of you who have helped make this dream possible.

Much of what I have learned over the years has come as the result of being a father to two wonderful children, Myranda and Sarah, who, in their own ways, inspired me and subconsciously contributed a tremendous amount to the content of this book. A little bit of each of them will be found here weaving in and out of the pages—thanks kids!

I would also like to thank a group of individuals with amazing talent. They have dedicated endless hours of their time, knowledge, ideas, and numerous tips—all of which culminated in the completion of this book. So to Clare Gilbert, Krista Bohr, Terri May, and Skip Morris, thank you for everything and most of all, thank you for your friendship.

Always,
D.C. Akers

HAVEN

REVENGE OF THE VIPER

"A lie is but a whisper of the treachery yet to come."

— Sinister Bones

CHAPTER 1

The two cloaked men entered the hallway, their staffs in hand, eyes narrowed, and faces taut with worry. They acknowledged one another with a slight tilt of the head as they rounded a corner of the dimly lit corridor.

"Any word?" asked Vallen, the younger of the two.

"No, nothing," replied Demetrius.

Large ivory sconces burned with a low flame, casting elongated shadows across the red marble floor and down the center of the stone corridor. The two men marched in unison, their knee-high black boots echoing as they struck the ground and their long emerald-colored cloaks snapping at their feet.

"Was she on assignment?" asked Vallen, his gray eyes gleaming between flickers of light. He stood six feet tall and his features were rugged. He had high cheek bones, a thin nose, and a pronounced jaw line that swept back into his long brown hair. Demetrius, on the other hand, was much older but just as tall. His gray hair was short and unkempt. His facial features were softer than Vallen's with a kind familiarity about them.

Vallen, a Keeper for the last ten years, had not worked with Demetrius often; most of what he knew of Demetrius came from stories. Demetrius was a legend amongst the Keepers, known for his wisdom and power of the elements. He was a battle-hardened veteran and war hero. But like most heroes, that title had come with a price, one of personal loss and great tragedy. If Demetrius Lore was worried then the situation was definitely grim. Something had gone wrong. Terribly wrong.

"Demetrius?"

Demetrius turned and looked at Vallen for the first time since entering the hallway. Demetrius wore a blank expression.

"I'm sorry, what did you say?" he asked, rounding the next corner.

Two Centurions stood at their post mid-way down the corridor. They nodded as the two Keepers passed them. Draped in long, cobalt blue cloaks and silver armor, the Centurions were more than just soldiers; they were Majesty guards. Their elegant silver armor hung in layers, like thin overlapping leaves from their shoulders down to their arms. The Majesty Crest was centered on their breast plates, which were made of larger bands of silver metal wrapped vertically around their chest, down their torso, thighs, and calves. Their helmets featured large Falcon wings riveted to the front as well as nose and full cheek guards.

Each Centurion held a long silver staff with an exquisitely decorated pommel made of crushed sapphire and silver. The pommel was forged in the shape of the Majesty Crest.

Vallen and Demetrius approached the end of the corridor, which was dark except for the dim light from the two large caldrons that flanked the entrance to the Majesty chambers.

"I was asking if she was on assignment for the Majesty," Vallen said again. But Demetrius still did not answer. His solemn glare was one of confusion and emptiness. Finally, as they made their way down the massive staircase into the main hall, Demetrius answered.

"I know as much as you," he said abruptly. "I was in Bayville when I received the scroll. I was told it was urgent, that it regarded Holly, and to return to the Majesty at once."

So that's it, Vallen thought. *Demetrius is worried about Holly.* He nodded in agreement; he had received the same scroll. But for him, there was one difference—it was not personal.

The large hallway came to an end, opening into a grand room filled with statues of wild horses, ancient weapons, and a large ornate table made of bronze that stood in the center of the room. A centerpiece of five flickering purple flames hovered inches above the table and a perimeter of blue torches attached to magnificent stone pillars served as ambient light. Their glow illuminated the walls of the chamber, revealing elaborate rectangular carvings of white marble floating twenty feet above the ground. Inscribed on the carvings were the names of fallen soldiers who had given their lives protecting Haven's freedom.

The crest of the Majesty was magnificently carved on the center of the gray slate floor. It was a cobalt blue star with small black spheres outlined in silver between each point. Inside each sphere was the symbol for one of the Estates: a raven representing the Vampires, a mace for the Orcs, an arrow and shield for the Elves, and a crescent moon with three stars for the Witches. The fifth was the new addition to the Estates—a pair of crossed swords representing the Goblin race. The crest was encompassed in a thin silver band of unity.

The two men hurried into the chamber, discreetly proceeded to the back of the room and waited for the summit to begin. The Orcs and Elvin delegates were already seated, as were the Witches and Vampires.

Atamar von Bogdan, the Minister of Justice, stood in the center of the room with Bellisoria Vontella, the Witch High Priestess. Atamar was dressed in long black robes with sleeves that hung past his palms. His body was thin and gangly, and his bald head was oddly shaped, like a large egg. He had a long hooked nose and chestnut-colored eyes. The man resembled a large vulture more than a Minister of anything.

It didn't help matters that Atamar stood next to the lovely Bellisoria either. With her long, flowing black hair and creamy olive skin, she was a striking woman. Her beauty was timeless—no one outside Haven would have ever guessed that she was well over six hundred years old.

Bellisoria gazed politely around the room, nodding to acknowledge the other delegates. Her eyes, the color of honey, were mesmerizing, and her thick, full lips occasionally gave way to a kind smile that demanded attention.

Vallen scrutinized Atamar from the back of the room. Something was not right about the Minister, he surmised. Atamar's eyes shifted from side to side and he was fidgeting as he stood before the Majesty. His normal swagger and military bearing were all but gone. Bellisoria, on the other hand, stood poised, her demeanor as calm and collected as always. She was considered royalty by most, a queen by some, and the leader of the Majesty by all.

She was dressed in an elegant, slim-fitted, v-neck satin gown covered in lavender lace. A chapel-length train and covered buttons completed the elegant ensemble. A pendant of diamonds and amethyst hung from a silver chain around her neck. The glimmering pendant was fashioned in the shape of an eye, the symbol of her coven. An ornate silver sheath concealing her wand hung on a thin silver chain draped around her waist.

The Great Hall of the Majesty continued to bluster with its usual conversations of problems and situations that affected its leaders. Whispers of negotiations and commerce fluttered around the table like usual until a single voice rang out, silencing the Majesty leaders.

"Where are they?" asked one of the three Vampires.

Vallen recognized the vampire as Kellen Doru, the prelate for Lord Valteen. Like all vampires, Kellen's eyes were a light violet that glowed luminescent against his pale pallid skin.

"The Goblins, where are they?"

Kellen was tall and extremely menacing. His slick black hair lay flat across his forehead and swayed down the length of his long, thin neck. Like all the other vampires, he wore a long, black traveling cloak that draped loosely over one shoulder, covering most of his flat black armor and silver daggers.

The remaining Vampires sat quietly, their angelic faces motionless but stern. Vallen recognized Alexandria Roahand, the Vampire Priestess, who sat to the right of Kellen. She was known to be a proficient practitioner of black magic. Then there was Latrice Dramore, who stood towering behind them; he was a large, muscular Vampire known as a Warrior. Several of the Majesty looked around and nodded in obvious aggravation. No one cared for the Goblins and their greed, and no one despised them more than the Vampires, but Bellisoria had made it clear to the Majesty long ago that the Goblins could no longer be ignored. Their numbers were far too vast and were still growing. They had to be embraced now as an ally before the Goblins outnumbered them as their enemy.

The commotion came to an end when two small, heavy-set Goblins came bounding into the chamber. Their burgundy cloaks and brown leather armor were tattered and pale compared to the glamour of the rest of the Majesty. The Goblins were bestial in appearance and grotesquely disfigured. Their brows were fully covered with thick black hair, and their mouths were filled with jagged, yellowed, crooked teeth.

Several of the Majesty scoffed, pulling their cloaks closer to themselves in disgust at the sight of the newcomers. Even the Orcs, who were rather beastly themselves, looked appalled. It was quite apparent that the Goblins, with their beady yellow eyes and peasant-like qualities, were not welcome there, or anywhere else in Haven as far as everyone else was concerned.

"Sorry, sorry, our apologies, did we miss anything?" Tryson, the Goblin Ambassador asked anxiously as he hopped up into his seat. He looked around the table at his counterparts and was met with solemn stares. "Please, everyone, please, let's get started," Atamar began.

He looked over at Bellisoria, who gave him a faint smile. He stepped to one side and she walked gracefully to the front of the table, taking her place before the Realm of the Estates. Silence enveloped the room; all eyes were on their leader.

"Thank you all for coming. It's good to see each of you again." She graciously smiled as her gaze traveled across the leaders gathered in front of her. Then she took in a deep breath and continued.

"We have called this meeting to discuss a situation that has come to our attention, but before I turn things back over to the Minister of Justice, I would like to say a few words." She paused. The silence in the room was deafening.

"Sometimes in life it is important to remember the past so you can appreciate the present and plan for the future," she continued. "As leaders of the Estates we have an obligation to our people to never forget where we came from and the sacrifices that were made to get us here."

Her tone was calm but firm. She looked over at Atamar. Sweat was beginning to pool on his large brow. She turned back to the leaders and continued.

"Over six hundred years ago during the Great Witch Hunt on Earth, I escaped my captors and fled into the nearby forest. There, I happened upon a hidden cavern, and in that cavern I found a portal. I used this portal to reach Haven, which was uninhabited at the time. The planet was perfectly able to sustain life and was similar to Earth, so I brought forth the sisters of my coven."

The Witches of the North bowed their heads in gratitude as Bellisoria continued.

"But I did not stop there. I, in turn, offered sanctuary for every human, non-human, dead and undead; a place to call home, a safe haven for the supernatural."

Orcs pounded the table, Elves raised their glasses, and Witches nodded in agreement, but the Vampires and Goblins sat motionless.

"For many years it was just that—a haven, but like all worlds it had its secrets. The signs were ever so slight, but even in its infancy there was evil at its core. Over time the malice began to spread like a disease, infecting everything in its path.

"Eventually, epic wars of the supernatural broke out. Battles of greed, power, and religion began to consume Haven, and I watched my planet transform into the very world from which I had escaped long ago. Desperate to fight back, to bring justice to my once peaceful world, I convinced four of the largest factions to meet in secret, and there we negotiated a truce."

Cheers rang out and the great hall was energized; Bellisoria had their attention now. She needed this alliance to be stronger than ever.

"We agreed that it was in our best interest to work together before our world imploded. Together we stood a chance—divided we stood to lose everything," she continued. "After days of negotiations, the Majesty was established, made up of the Four Estates of the Realm: Vampires, Witches, Orcs, and Elves. Recently the Goblins were added to the Estates with the signing of the new zone treaty." She waved her hand in the direction of the Goblins who smirked in smug satisfaction.

"The Majesty took its place as the governing authority in Haven's political society. Since its establishment, many battles have been fought to protect our sacred way of life. We, the Majesty, now honor the sacrifices made by our comrades and loved ones with this alliance. Let us never forget the fallen who gave their lives so that we may have everything we want, but never want for anything we may need." Bellisoria's eyes narrowed. "Let nothing tear us apart."

The Majesty stood to their feet clapping and cheering; even the Vampires and Goblins were standing now. Bellisoria looked on with a strained smile, surveying the room. She knew that over the years life in Haven had changed; the once powerful alliances had become frayed and fragile. Hope had been replaced with despair, courage with fear, and honor with deception. Everyone had their own agenda now, and greed was the root cause. In these grave times Bellisoria trusted very few. With a handful of advisors and her most trusted Keeper Agents at her side, she bore the daunting task of seeing beyond the trickery and secret coalitions to bring peace back to the lands of Haven.

Still smiling, she motioned for Atamar, who took her place in front of the large table, applauding her as she moved aside. After a few minutes when the room had quieted down and everyone had taken their seats again, Atamar cleared his throat and began.

"First, I would like to thank each and every one of you for coming on such short notice, but I assure you, the matter we have to discuss is one of great importance and it affects us all. Let it be known that this information is of the highest secrecy, and under no circumstances can it be divulged to anyone beyond your senior cabinet members."

The Realm representatives looked around at one another and shifted uncomfortably in their chairs.

"Let me repeat," his tone was stern. "Under no circumstances can this information be divulged to anyone beyond your senior cabinet members." Atamar took a moment to let his words linger in the air before speaking again.

"As you well know, thirteen years ago we all fought in the Great War against Cyrus Kan, the Emperor of the Dark Lands. To our credit, we freed many captives from prison camps and destroyed several Viper breeding facilities. But that victory came with our share of losses. We all suffered great casualties in that war, and we lost a great leader in Rylan Dalcome."

Several of the members nodded in agreement. No one knew what had really happened to Rylan that day. He was separated from the other Keeper Agents in battle and was later found dead in a remote area of the prison camp. Some speculated that he died in battle fighting three Banshees single-handedly, some believed his death was a conspiracy the Majesty had covered up, but no one really knew what happened that day, not even Demetrius.

Atamar raised his hands to gather the group's attention once more before continuing.

"With that said, it pains me to inform you that our battle did not end with the Great War as we had hoped." Voices erupted in whispers around the room.

"Less than three days ago, the Majesty received word that three of our Keeper Agents patrolling the Blackfoot mountains were attacked by—" The words stuck in his throat.

The room fell silent, the Realm delegates waited in anticipation. Atamar took in a long deliberate breath and sighed.

"A Viper."

Chapter 2

Sam was running as fast as he could. Sarah was calling him. The beast was right behind him. He tried but he couldn't run any faster. He could feel the creature's hot breath on the back of his neck. If he stopped now he would be trampled, crushed by the monster behind him.

Trees sped by in a blur. The moon was his only compass but Sam was almost there; he could see the opening in the tree line at the top of hill. The moon was the brightest he had even seen, casting white, radiant bands of light in all directions. In the center of the clearing stood the silhouette of a girl. It was his sister, it was Sarah!

Sam jerked, and rolled out of bed and onto the floor. He landed with a loud thud and his eyes flung open. He was lying face down, staring into the dark wooden floor.

"Ugh," he grunted. "That hurt."

He looked around as his vision slowly came into focus. The sun was shining brightly into his room even though the blinds were closed. The first things that came into focus were his sneakers, which were still wet from the caves. They were covered in bird droppings and smelled horrible. He turned away from his sneakers and saw his ear buds that were under his bed. He had been looking for those. Sam craned his head up to see the side of his bed. His body was cold and covered in sweat again, like it always was after his dreams. His muscles ached; the pain ran across his shoulders and down his back. The scratches and scrapes along his torso, arms, and legs still stung from the night before.

Sam rolled over onto his back and pulled the comforter down from the bed on top of him. His breathing and heartbeat were still elevated. *It was just a dream,* he told himself. *It didn't mean anything.* But he wasn't sure about that anymore. A few days ago there had been no magic in the world. But now everything had changed. Magic was real—he and Travis had seen it with their own eyes. *Nothing will ever be the same again,* he told himself. Everything had the possibility of being something more than it seemed.

The world had changed overnight. The impossible had become possible, and now his world was a much bigger place. It made him feel small and insignificant, even more so than usual. And that scared Sam. He was living in a place where people could vanish into thin air and objects could literally levitate for no apparent reason. *That's not right,* he told himself. That went against everything that was humanly possible. Or did it?

Maybe it was time to tell his mother. After all, it wouldn't be just him now trying to convince her of the impossible. Travis would be his witness—he had seen it all. Travis had seen the spiders and the floating mirror at the caves. They could tell his mother about the stranger and how he disappeared. Sam stopped and thought for a moment. It all sounded crazy even as he listened to it himself. She would never believe them.

Sam's head was beginning to hurt. He didn't want to think about this anymore. Lifting himself straight, he felt a sharp pain across his ribcage. Gradually, he stood, placing his hand on his back as if he were a ninety-year-old man. At least he had slept through most of the night before having the dream, although it would have been nice to have slept in for a change.

Sam grabbed a shirt and a pair of shorts from the closet and put them on. He didn't bother to turn on a light since the morning sun was so bright. Instead, he opened both windows in his room. First he opened the window that faced the street, and then the one that faced his new neighbor. To his surprise, the girl was standing at her window again. Her long black hair was pulled to one side and her jade-colored eyes stared directly back at him as if she had been waiting for him. She was dressed in a white t-shirt and shorts. Sam hesitated at first, but managed to give a slight wave. The girl stood motionless for a brief moment, then the right corner of her mouth curled upward ever so slightly into a half-smile.

Sam, who was beginning to feel more confident, willed a smile of his own when the blinds of her window abruptly snapped shut. Sam's smile quickly faded. He stood frozen, except for his hand that was still waving.

Wow, that could have gone better. He sighed, turned, and grabbed his cell phone from the dresser and his ear buds from the floor.

When Sam returned to the window he saw that Giddyup Lane was busy with neighbors. He looked out and saw people walking their dogs, Teddy riding his bike, and Mrs. Cambridge tending to her yard. Sam loved being out of school and knowing that he had nothing to do, expect for whatever he wanted. That made him smile.

Sam made his way down the stairs and into the kitchen where he noticed a small yellow note stuck to the counter.

Sam,

> *Do not forget to clean out the garage like we talked about. Goodwill will be coming tomorrow to pick up the boxes of old clothes so have them ready to go near the front of the garage. Remember, I need you and Sarah to help out this summer, so make sure you do all your chores. I had to open this morning at the diner but I will see you when I get home.*
>
> *Mom*

"Great," he sighed, "more cleaning."

He hated to clean, but his mom needed the help. Besides, since he couldn't get a job to help her out, this was probably the next best thing.

It wasn't long before Sarah made her way down the stairs. Her long brown hair was pulled back into a tight pony tail. She was wearing a gray tank top, matching shorts, and was barefoot.

Sam had already made up his mind that he was not going to make any of the Dalcome women cry today. As bad as the last few days had been the last thing he needed was the bitter and sarcastic resentment the Dalcome women were famous for once they had been scorned. No, that was a mistake he would not make twice in a row.

"Good morning," Sam said, trying his best to be cheerful.

Sarah didn't even look at him as she walked directly to the pantry and pulled out a loaf of bread.

"What's so good about it?" she replied in a monotone voice.

She was obviously still mad at him for yesterday's little outbreak of word vomit in which he had told his extremely annoying, yet apparently very fragile older sister to shut up. That had gone over like a lead balloon. He had expected her to fight back, but instead she had said nothing. Even worse, she had cried. Not like a boo-hoo cry, but like a sin-gle-tear-you-hurt-my-feelings kind of cry, and who can deal with that?

"Um, I was going to make us some breakfast, if you want some?" This was Sam's first attempt at a peace offering.

"I'm not hungry," she snapped while removing two piec-es of bread from the plastic bag. Sam smiled briefly.

"Well, it looks like you might be a little hungry," he said, his tone still cheerful.

Sarah twisted the bread bag into a tight knot and shoved it back into the pantry. What was once a large loaf of bread now looked more like a small dinner roll. She whipped her pony tail around and walked over to the large kitchen win-dow where Barron was waiting like he did every morning. She flung the window open and threw out the two pieces of bread. She then slammed the window shut and whipped her head back around to face Sam.

"Satisfied?"

Her face was red and her eyes glared back at him. Sam actually thought he might laugh. She looked like a cartoon character who was about to blow steam out of her ears. But he didn't. He knew that would throw a big wrench in the whole *I'm not going to make any of the Dalcome women cry today* plan.

Sarah waited for a moment, expecting Sam to make some kind wise crack, but he didn't.

"Okay ... well, I thought I would ask," he said politely.

Sarah scoffed, then turned and left the room. Sam looked out the window at Barron as he bit into the first piece of bread.

"Well, that didn't go well," he said to Barron, who licked his lips.

For most of the day Sam did his best to avoid Sarah so as to not make things worse between them. Not to mention it was safer to steer clear of her because of the mood she was in. They both did their chores; Sam did everything outside, which included de-weeding the flower beds, mowing, and edging. Sarah did everything indoors like dusting and vacuuming. Whenever Sarah wasn't working she was constantly yelling on her phone with Barry. There was obviously something wrong in Sarahland and the queen was not happy!

Travis called at about noon to tell Sam he would be over later; they had a lot to talk about with regards to the previous night. Sam also wanted to let him know about his dream he had again. But before any of that could happen he had one chore left—the garage. This was going to be a beating of epic proportion, he could just feel it.

Sam reluctantly made his way out the back door of the house to the gray and white garage that was nestled between two large oak trees. A rusted handle hung loosely on the weather-beaten door. The door itself had sporadic patches of brown wood where the paint had fallen off. The wood looked old and fragile, no doubt from wood rot.

Sam reached for the handle, lifting it up to raise the door. The dilapidated wood creaked and the springs twanged as they recoiled. Sam quickly let go of the handle and the rickety door gradually slid up and out of view.

A wave of hot, humid air hit Sam square in the face. The smell of dust and cardboard boxes vanquished every molecule of fresh air around him. He stood there amazed. It had been some time since he had been out to the garage and what the hell happened in here?

"Epic," he sighed.

The garage was a twenty-by-twenty giant cluster of chaos with tons of old boxes, bikes, yard equipment, lawn chairs, and countless other things.

This is going to be a life-sucking event, Sam thought. How in the world was he going to move all this crap around? *And they thought my room was a mess? Give me a break.* This was going to take forever. What if there were spiders in there, the same spiders from last night? Man, he didn't even want to think about that.

This was a horrible way to start the summer. But maybe he deserved it. *Maybe this is what they call bad karma,* he wondered. *Maybe this is what happens when you tick off your mom and your sister in the same weekend!*

Even with the garage door open, there was very little breeze inside. It felt like a bad sauna in a spa from hell. Sam found a rusty floor fan that barely worked. It squeaked and rattled as its blades slowly turned, throwing out more dust than air.

Sam worked vigorously for hours with his ear buds in, shuffling music from old 80's rock to the latest top 40. He thought of the last few days, the magic he knew existed, and the stranger that had disappeared. They were connected somehow, he just knew it. But how?

Four-and-a-half-hours later, Sam was finally done. He stood at the front of the garage examining his work. It was funny—for something he hated doing so much, he was really quite good at cleaning.

All the boxes for Goodwill were neatly stacked at the front of the garage, the lawn equipment was organized to the side, and the bikes were hung up on hooks from the rafters. Baseballs, picture frames, and old Hot Wheels had been thrown in a few empty paint buckets along the back wall. Sam put the remaining clutter in neat piles on the curb for tomorrow's trash pickup.

The only thing left to do was turn off the fan, sweep the floor, and call it a day. Sam was walking back into the garage to grab the broom that was leaning in the corner when he noticed a small panel that had been dislodged from the wall near the floor. He walked closer, pulling his ear buds out, and knelt down next to the small opening.

Sam grasped the wooden panel and moved it to the side. Behind the panel, tucked neatly away between the two wooden wall studs, was a book. But it was not just any book; it was a book with four golden symbols. Four symbols he had recently seen before: Earth, Water, Air, and Fire.

Chapter 3

The word Viper hung in the air as the Majesty stared back at Atamar in utter shock. Eyes darted around the room in quiet panic. Fear fell like a plague upon them, seizing every ounce of their courage. Then several of the Vampires stood, followed by the Orcs and Witches and the quiet room exploded into pandemonium. An upheaval of protest erupted around the table, and multiple questions clamored together into one congested voice.

"Holly," Demetrius gasped, "It was Holly! She was one of the Keepers who had been attacked!" Demetrius looked over at Vallen, who had come to the same conclusion.

Vallen could only imagine what was going through Demetrius's head. Holly was one of his own, one that he had trained since she was a child, just like Rylan Dalcome. Now, she too had been killed.

Atamar tried frantically to regain control over the meeting but his voice was lost in the outcries of the angry leaders.

"Please ... please ... I need your attention!" he yelled. But no one was listening. Vampires were now yelling at Goblins,

Elves and Witches were yelling at Orcs. This was the very outburst that Atamar had been trying to avoid.

Suddenly, without warning, a loud crack rang out like a whip, echoing through the Grand Hall. With a loud, thundering roar, purple flames exploded into the chamber and billowed across the ceiling, traveling down the walls before evaporating into tiny sparks on the ground.

"Silence!" Bellisoria shouted, her silver wand held high above her head.

The commotion ceased at once. For a moment the leaders stood motionless, completely stunned. This was out of character for Bellisoria. On many occasions she had been the voice of reason, the calm in the storm. But tonight she seemed to be on edge. Tonight there was a sense of urgency in her voice. The Realm of the Estates quietly took their seats. All eyes were focused on Bellisoria.

"I need each of you to listen," she said firmly. Her eyes moved around the room. The leaders were scared, angry, and confused, just as she knew they would be. She lowered her wand and slowly slipped it back into its silver sheath.

"Tell us then, Bellisoria, tell us what has happened," Elessar, the Elvin King, said. He was clearly trying to keep his composure.

"It is as Atamar said—we have received confirmation of a Viper. At the moment we are not sure how many there are."

"I don't understand. How can this be? We killed them— we killed them all many years ago," Elessar continued, his gray eyes pleading with the Witch.

"Bellisoria, could there be more?" asked Braya, the High

Priestess of the Eastern Coven and Principal of Hecate Academy of Witches.

"We are not sure, Braya," Bellisoria replied.

Then Alexandria stood to her feet, her violet eyes bearing down on Bellisoria.

"Well, apparently you have not been sure about a great many things. Bellisoria, correct me if I am wrong, but isn't Blackfoot the location of the last remaining portal?"

Bellisoria did not like Alexandria's tone and her golden eyes narrowed with irritation.

"Yes, that is correct. But as you all know it was deactivated many years ago," she said, directing her attention back to the other leaders.

"So you say," interrupted Tobias, the Goblin King. Bellisoria turned to face him. Tobias met her gaze, and his lips curled into a horrific smile, exposing his small yellow teeth. "But we really don't know that for sure, do we? I mean, you never found the gate keys. It was assumed that they were destroyed during the battle, along with the thieves. Right, Bellisoria? So how do we know for sure that the portal is deactivated? All we really have is the word of an Orc who supposedly searched the bodies," he said, relaxing back into his chair. It was obvious he was getting some sort of enjoyment out of this line of questioning.

Cantor, the Orc King, stood up and slammed his fist on the table. Even his cloak and armor could not conceal the huge muscles that rippled throughout his arms. Cantor was massive. He was a staggering seven feet tall and as wide as two grown men, so when he stood he took up a great amount of space in the chamber. Like all Orcs, he was bowlegged and long-armed with ashen skin and a snout-like nose. He had an immense head with slanted red eyes and pointed ears.

"What are you saying, Goblin? Are you calling me a liar?" Cantor asked, his voice deep and stern. He snapped his broad jaw threateningly to expose a host of terrible fangs and sharp teeth.

"No, no, come now," Tobias said in his sly tone. "I am merely suggesting that you might have made an error. I mean after all, you did think the Vipers were all but extinct and you were wrong about that. I'm simply pointing out that what you assumed and what we now know are two vastly different things. Someone, or in your case, something, got it wrong. That's all."

Cantor's eyes narrowed and the veins in his thick neck began to bulge.

"How dare you speak to me like that, you filthy Goblin!" he roared, pounding his fists on the table again. "You were not there! You did not stand and fight, you coward! You did not spill your blood to make the way safe! We searched the dead and found no keys!"

Vallen did not like where this was going. Cantor was furious and he was known for his temper. The Goblin needed to keep his mouth shut, Vallen thought.

Tobias leaned forward. His yellow eyes were slits now. "I assure you, Orc, had we been there we would not be sitting here today wondering why there are still Vipers running loose." Suddenly, Tobias stood from his chair and they both reached for their swords.

"Enough, both of you!" Bellisoria yelled. She and Atamar

withdrew their wands simultaneously and pointed them directly at Cantor. Vallen and Demetrius had already emerged from the shadows, brandishing their staffs in Tobias's direction.

"Sit down and sheath your weapons! We have far greater problems at hand!" Bellisoria commanded. "And Tobias, it would be wise of you to hold your tongue. Many Orcs, and countless others, died in the Great War. Assigning blame will not bode well for you here. I suggest you refrain from those kinds of accusations. Do I make myself clear?" she asked with a contemptuous look on her face.

Cantor and Tobias slowly slid their swords back into their sheaths, but their eyes remained fixed on one another as they gradually sat down.

Tobias slowly leaned back into his chair, his snarling face fading into a roguish smile as he turned his attention to Bellisoria again.

"Yes, but of course, Bellisoria, as you wish."

Bellisoria and Atamar stowed their wands. Seeing this, Demetrius and Vallen followed suit, lowering their staffs and stepping back into the shadows of the chamber.

"I recommend that we close the borders and ports to our domains," Braya said, her eyes shifting back and forth between Goblin and Orc.

"I agree. We must keep travel down to a minimum," said Elessar. "We know how they feed, so maybe we can starve them to death."

Bellisoria winced at the memory of seeing the Vipers feeding on the flesh of the fallen soldiers in the breeding camps during the war.

"No, that will not work," Cantor said, still glaring at Tobias. "Vipers take what they want, and we can do little to stop them."

"How could this have happened? We were so careful!" Varah, the Northern Witch Ambassador, said.

"I don't know, but we need to proceed cautiously," said Bellisoria. "We still need more information."

"Yes ... we do, Bellisoria. We need the truth," boomed a voice.

The Realm leaders sat at attention, startled by the noise that seemed to have come from all directions. The voice was ominous, yet soothing and seductive. The leaders looked around the room searching for its origin.

"I'm sorry?" Bellisoria asked apprehensively. Her eyes cautiously scanned the room with the others.

Demetrius and Vallen searched the room too, peering through the shadows of the torch light, but the voice seemed to surround them, and come from nowhere.

"Come now, you know more than you speak of, Bellisoria. Please do not insult us further. And tell us of Alisa," the voice said. The speaker's words seemed to roll off his tongue with a slow agonizing elegance.

Vallen's eyes narrowed. *Alisa—what did she have to do with any of this? She was dead. She and her family had died long ago.* Vallen looked over at Demetrius, who was no longer searching for the mysterious voice but instead was focused on Bellisoria.

Bellisoria knew that voice, that regal tone, that unmistakable serene demeanor; it could be none other than Valteen, Lord of the Vampires. It had been ages since

Valteen attended a Majesty Summit personally; he always sent his prelate, Kellen, and other members of the coven in his place. But now, from the dark recesses of the room, a large silhouette stretched across the fire-lit floor. In the distance Lord Valteen stood with his sword drawn. He stabbed at the glowing embers inside the handsome stone fireplace at the back of the room.

Bellisoria did not speak. Her face became flushed; not because of Valteen, but because of his line of questioning—specifically his question about Alisa. She was stunned, and she knew the look on her face betrayed her. Bellisoria searched for the right words, some quick-witted rebuttal, but none came. The rest of the Majesty looked on, staring in silence, waiting for her to answer.

"What?" she gasped. Her voice trembled slightly when she spoke and her head swam with emotion. *This is it, this is it,* she told herself. Valteen knew, somehow—he knew what it was she had been hiding all these years, and he was going to get it out of her one way or another in front of the entire Majesty.

There would be no hiding it this time. The five estates would not forgive such betrayal and the secret would destroy hundreds of years of peace between the races. It would be the last day of the alliance, the last day of the Majesty.

"What is he talking about, Bellisoria?" Elessar asked. His voice was much more urgent now. The fire roared as Valteen continued to stab into the open flame.

"If the Viper is in the Blackfoot Mountains, there is only one reason it is there. And we both know what that is, don't we, Bellisoria?" Valteen said.

Bellisoria stood motionless. She looked down now at the table, staring into her reflection.

"Bellisoria, please say something," Braya pleaded.

"What? No clever answer? No sarcastic reply from our high priestess?" Valteen chided, his violet gaze cutting through the darkness like the eyes of a demon.

Atamar, who was still perspiring, slid his right hand beneath his robes and slowly grasped the handle of his wand again. The Vampire King slowly emerged from the shadows. His long black hair fell past his square jaw line and violet-colored eyes shimmered like glass against his gaunt, colorless face. He was dressed in a long, black crimson-trimmed cloak, fastened by a silver chain with talon clasps. He moved gracefully, like a Wraith to its prey, his sword now sheathed. He walked behind Bellisoria and with a soft perspicacious tone whispered, "Answer the question."

"Hold your tongue, Valteen!" Atamar said.

Valteen's head whipped around, his long white fangs exposed, "No, Atamar, it's time—time we all know your little secret!"

"The Dalcomes are dead! Tell him, Bellisoria, tell him!" Elessar said standing to his feet.

Bellisoria looked up, her face riddled with shame. *There is no way out,* she thought. *No way out.*

"No Elessar," she said taking a breath, "I cannot say that, for they are not all dead."

Great gasps of disbelief filled the air and the Majesty began to whisper again. Vallen's jaw dropped. *What, alive? That's impossible,* he thought. He looked to Demetrius, expecting to see shock on his face, but to his surprise it wasn't there. In fact, Demetrius looked sad, disappointed even. *But that couldn't be. He was close to the Dalcomes. They were like family to him. Unless,* Vallen contemplated, *unless Demetrius knew she was alive and that she was hiding.* Vallen's eyes narrowed. *Yes, that's it. Demetrius knew—he had known all along.*

Demetrius remained stoic, careful not to show any reaction to this unfortunate development. *How did the Vampires find out? Who would have divulged this information?*

"What, I ... I ... don't understand, Bellisoria, what are you saying?" Elessar asked.

"Isn't it obvious, Elf? She lied to you," Tobias said smugly.

Bellisoria tried to regain her composure. She took a deep breath and focused her attention on Elessar.

"Yes, I suppose that is one way to look at it," she said calmly. Then she turned her attention to Valteen, who was making his way around the room to the other Vampires. "What do you want to know?" she asked.

Atamar stepped forward shaking his head. "No, No, we can't." But Bellisoria raised her hand, signaling for his silence.

"High Priestess, no!" Atamar pleaded. But her solemn eyes met his.

"It's time Atamar. It's time they knew." Atamar opened his mouth to speak again but he abruptly stopped. He could see the conviction in her eyes and he knew there was nothing he could say to change her mind.

"It's time," Bellisoria said once more. This time her look was one of understanding for she knew the great lengths they had taken to keep this secret safe.

She turned and faced Valteen.

"Where is Alisa Dalcome?" Valteen snapped, his Romanian accent more apparent now.

"She is on Earth," Bellisoria responded coldly.

The Majesty broke out in another uproar as they all stood from their seats. Even the Witches were standing now. But Bellisoria held her ground, her glare focused on Valteen. Demetrius and Vallen stepped out from the shadows once more to Bellisoria's side as the Centurion Guards made their way into the chamber and fanned out around the perimeter of the great hall.

"Silence!" Valteen yelled, his voice reverberating off the chamber walls. He waited as the hall fell quiet once more and the Realm leaders took their seats. Once everything was quiet again, Valteen continued his line of questioning.

"And when did she travel to Earth?" he asked. Bellisoria's eyes were still fixed on him as she answered.

"Thirteen years ago."

Suddenly Elessar stood again. His gray eyes were like slits hidden beneath his furrowed brow. The High Elves were greatly respected, not only because of their wisdom but because of their ability to gather intelligence.

Bellisoria knew Elessar would take this information as a betrayal because of their close relationship. Over the years, Elessar had become her confidant and dear friend. Elessar had mentored Bellisoria long ago in the values of leadership. He had pressed upon her the importance of vision, principle, honor, valor, courage, and humility. All the qualities she would need to possess if she were to become the leader Haven would one day need. *What does he think of me now,* she wondered.

"Please Bellisoria, explain," he said. "Explain why you have kept this from us for so long." Elessar was trying to help her; that much she knew. He was trying to give her an opportunity to explain her bizarre behavior—to make sense of what Valteen was accusing her of, and to prove to him that he had not put his trust in the wrong person. But the truth was he had. Even though what she had done was more for the good of Haven and less for their leaders, she still had betrayed him by not being forthcoming. The leaders of the Realm tended to have their own agendas and they were not always in the best interest of the people. She had just wanted to give her friend's family a second chance and a new life.

Bellisoria sighed. She looked at Elessar, her remorseful eyes catching his, as if to convey how deeply sorry she was for keeping this from him. But it was something that had to be done.

"Alisa was sent to Earth thirteen years ago as a sleeper agent. She went with the keys to all four portals." Her eyes moved around the room as the Majesty leaders looked on in disbelief.

"But you said that the other three were destroyed! You said there was only one that remained, and it was no longer functional," Elessar said.

"You don't understand. It was not safe to keep the keys here. It was not safe for any of us," Bellisoria pleaded.

"But that was a decision that should have been made by the Majesty!" said Kellen.

"No!" she said abruptly. "It was a decision I had to make alone. Only I know where the other portals lead. They lead to worlds far worse than we can imagine. They are inhabited by monstrous fiends capable of unspeakable evil and destruction like nothing we have ever seen before. No, I could not leave it up to the Majesty to vote. It was my burden to bear, it was my decision to make, and I did."

"What did you do, Bellisoria?" Valteen interjected. His voice was cold and his glare unrelenting.

Bellisoria swallowed hard and continued her story.

"After the death of Rylan Dalcome, we approached Alisa with the opportunity to travel to Earth as a sleeper agent. It would also provide a new start for her and her family. It was obvious, considering her vital role in the downfall of Cyrus Kan's army, that she and her children would be a target for future attacks. At that time, we explained to her that she had only one mission, and that was to hide and protect the portal keys. She left with her children and the eleven portal keys."

"Eleven? Why eleven? That seems like an odd number," Tobias prodded. He was sitting up straight now, his interest piqued.

Bellisoria turned to Tobias, knowing what his true intentions were. He was like the rest of Realm leaders, with the exception of the Witches and perhaps the Elves, whom she trusted. All the others wanted the gate keys for themselves. They wanted the opportunity to do what Bellisoria had done, to discover an uninhabited world and rule it for themselves. But Bellisoria could not let that happen. She had been to both the Air and Fire worlds and she had barely made it back alive. Haven, the Water world, and Earth were the only two of the elemental planets safe enough to colonize.

"Each portal creates a time rift that requires three keys to operate it; one to travel through, and two to return," she explained.

"So, where is the missing key? There should be twelve," Alexandria said.

"The last key is safe. We use it to send scrolls to Earth though the portal; this is how we communicate with Alisa. It is not possible to send a scroll to another planet without opening a portal."

Valteen was pacing back and forth as he listened to Bellisoria intently. Then he stopped and turned to the Witch.

"So, what has our sleeper agent been up to for the last thirteen years?" he asked. His tone oozed with arrogance. Bellisoria's glare returned to Valteen. She hated the self-righteous Vampire, and hated him even more for taking pleasure at her expense.

"She and her family are well," she said indignantly. "She has settled into a normal human life. Her days of the Majesty are all but over."

"And the keys—what of the keys?" asked Tobias.

"They are safe, as safe as they have been for thirteen long years," Bellisoria replied.

"This is an outrage! You have lied to us, Bellisoria, and you have lied to the Realms!" Cantor said. His accusation cut deeply, but Bellisoria knew it was true. Cantor was right. She had lied, but there had been no other way.

"Cantor, you must understand it was for our own good. I did it to protect us," she said, trying desperately to make her point.

"No, it was good for you, the Witches and your select few, but not for us!" he replied. "You wanted the other worlds for yourself as you did with Haven!"

"That is not true! I brought you here!" she exclaimed.

"You brought us here to rule over us!"

He turned to his second-in-command. "Come," he said. "I've heard enough. We leave!" The group of massive Orcs stood, pushing over their chairs, and stormed out of the Majesty chamber.

Elessar was next to stand, his regal features more apparent now in his anger. He stared at Bellisoria as if he were looking at her for the first time. It made her feel small, like a child about to be scolded.

"Bellisoria, we trusted you and you betrayed us. You betrayed me," he said. Bellisoria could hear not only the disappointment in his voice, but the pain as well. She had hurt Elessar; she had hurt her dear friend with her lies and deception.

"There is much to consider now," he continued. "You know better than anyone, Bellisoria that it takes years to build trust, but only one lie to undo it all."

Elessar and the other Elvin Ambassadors gathered their things quietly and left the room. She watched as Elessar walked away. The emptiness she felt inside was almost unbearable.

The remaining Majesty members looked on as Valteen approached the table once again.

"All good things must come to an end, and your time has come, Bellisoria," he said, and with a smug grin he turned to the other Vampires. "We go," he said. With that the Vampires stood and followed Valteen out of the chamber.

The Goblins, on the other hand, had not moved. In fact, Tobias had reached into his vest pocket and removed a small pipe. He filled it with tobacco and lit the pipe with one of the small floating flames in front of him.

"If I had to guess, that did not go as planned," he said to Bellisoria.

His lack of respect infuriated Vallen, Demetrius, and Atamar, and they all stepped forward at once but Bellisoria held up her hand. "Wait, let him speak."

Tobias smiled his hideous smile and puffed his pipe.

"You are going to need allies my Queen; you will need allies in numbers, vast numbers."

"What are you saying, Goblin?" Atamar asked.

Tobias removed the pipe from his mouth. "What I'm saying, Wizard, is that the Goblins will be at your service, should you call upon us."

Bellisoria tilted her head to one side and narrowed her eyes in thought. "At what cost?" she asked.

Tobias hopped from his chair to the floor; Tryson did the same. They both turned and began to leave.

"At what cost?" Bellisoria asked again, clearly agitated now.

Tobias stopped before turning the corner into the corridor and smiled. "For a fair price, but of course," he said, then turned and left.

She watched carefully as the Goblins left the chamber, then turned to Demetrius and Vallen. She sighed and gathered her thoughts.

"I'm glad you're here," she said with a faint smile.

"How did Valteen find out?" Demetrius asked. He looked back and forth between Bellisoria and Atamar.

"I don't know, but it confirms our suspicions that we have a spy amongst our agents."

"Atamar, what of Holly, is she okay?" Demetrius asked.

Bellisoria placed her hand on Demetrius's shoulder and her eyes met his.

"It was not Holly who was killed, Demetrius."

"Killed?" Vallen asked.

"Yes, there were two Keeper Agents, Dante and Atticus, who were sent to the Blackfoot Mountains to send the monthly communication to Alisa," Atamar said. "Somehow they were followed into the mountains and attacked. When they didn't report in I assembled another team to investigate—Xavier and Gordon. Atticus was already dead when they got there and they found Dante barely alive. He was critically injured and barely able to speak. He said it was a Viper. The portal to Earth had already been activated. Dante said he lay there unable to move, but that he had seen something pass through the portal. After hearing this I updated Xavier and Gordon regarding the Dalcomes and sent them to Earth. Asha's team arrived on the scene shortly after and recovered Dante and Atticus, then returned to the Majesty. Dante later died in the infirmary, so that is all we know."

Bellisoria could see the remorse in Vallen's eyes. He knew Dante and Atticus well; they had served together as a unit during the Great War.

"When Holly returned to the Majesty a day later I sent her to Earth as well. They were all given specific instructions to observe and not interact with the Dalcomes."

"What? Why? We need to warn Alisa!" Demetrius said. His glare was centered on Atamar as he spoke.

"Demetrius, I share your concern," Bellisoria interrupted. "But we are not sure what we are dealing with here. We cannot warn Alisa of something we are not sure of. There is too much at stake. Her children know nothing of this world; we could do more harm than good if we are wrong. Can you imagine the impact it would have on the Dalcome children to know their whole life has been nothing more than a cover-up to keep them safe? That everything they know about themselves and their parents is a lie?"

Demetrius stared at Bellisoria. His face was flushed, and his teeth clenched. Bellisoria took a step closer to him and met his gaze. Her voice was softer now, and her words were tender. "I know what they meant to you, Demetrius. I too lost a great friend in Rylan Dalcome, and trust me when I say the last thing I want to do is to see his family harmed. But, for their sake we must be sure; we must know what we are dealing with before we act. I promised Rylan I would keep his family safe, and I have no intention of breaking that promise now."

Demetrius's gaze slowly drifted from Bellisoria's eyes to the floor and he nodded in agreement.

"When can we leave?" Vallen asked.

All heads turned to Atamar.

"Now. Asha and her team will be waiting for you at the portal. Should there really be a Viper on Earth, you are to retrieve the Dalcomes and return home with them. They will be safer here at the Majesty than alone on Earth with only a handful of Keepers."

"Will Asha and her team be coming?" Vallen asked.

"No," Atamar replied. "Not now with the Realms in chaos. We will need every Keeper Agent we have left to protect the Majesty and the portal. If I know Valteen, tonight was but a glimpse of a much larger plan."

CHAPTER 4

Sam stared at the book for a brief moment before reaching down into the wall and removing it from its hiding place. It was surprisingly heavy for its size, which was probably due to the four gold medallions embedded in the cobalt leather cover.

The medallions were arranged in a circle in the center of the book; each was engraved with one of the four elemental signs: Earth, Water, Air, and Fire. The book was bound with a large clasp made of gold and silver ivy that traced elegantly around the cover, connecting in the middle to a large leaf-shaped lock with a small sapphire at its center. Sam had never seen a book like this before; it looked extremely old and foreign. The leather was soft and worn with small slender cracks that ran vertically down the cover.

He held the book in one hand and gently ran his fingers over the Water symbol. To his surprise, a small beam of light sprang from the symbol and encircled the Water crest. Sam trembled with excitement. The shear brilliance of the light was overwhelming. He had seen something similar to this back in the caves with the mirror, but this—this was incredible! To be so close, to be holding it in his hands, to *hold magic,* was nothing short of amazing! It made him feel like a superhero. No, it was more than that—it made him feel special and that was something Sam had never felt before.

As the book glowed, the luminescent Water symbol, with its rolling waves encircled by two thick bands, appeared between the rafters on the garage ceiling. Sam gazed up at it and could not help but smile. *Magic is awesome.* But at the same time, the symbol projected on the ceiling made him more than a little nervous. Magic had not turned out so well for him in the past, back in the caves with the floating mirror and the spiders. But the light coming from the book was so mesmerizing and overwhelming that Sam couldn't help but be intrigued. Magic was real and he was holding it in his hands. He couldn't stop now, he wanted to know more; he had to know more, and now was his chance.

Sam looked back down at the book and moved his finger to the next medallion. He touched it softly and, like the Water sign, it also began to glow, casting another image on the ceiling. This symbol was of three swirling gusts of wind that, to Sam, looked like fancy number nines. He knew this was the symbol for Air.

He continued this process until the symbols from all four medallions were glowing on the ceiling above him. Sam sat there, eyes wide in amazement, taking it all in. He was looking at something truly phenomenal, something most people only dreamed about, and he was holding it in his hands. As he reveled in the moment, he noticed that the images were beginning to fade in and out. He held the book tighter and gave it a light shake but it didn't seem to help, and to Sam's dismay the symbols abruptly disappeared from the ceiling.

He looked down and saw that the small sapphire at the center of the lock had begun to glow. Gradually, the faint blue became brighter and brighter until Sam had to turn away from the light and cover his eyes. The entire garage was now illuminated with the magnificent glow.

Sam slowly turned back around, giving his eyes time to adjust to the light. Still holding the book tightly, he looked down at the sapphire stone. His eyes shimmered with the magnificence of the scene before him and his breath caught in his chest as he felt a wave of anticipation swell up inside of him. The light was so intriguing, so inviting to Sam, but most of all, it was familiar. He didn't know how or why. He couldn't explain it—it just was. He felt the light pulling at something inside of him, drawing out a part of him that wanted or needed to connect with it. Sam gripped the book tightly. His hands started to tingle in expectancy and his muscles were tense. He felt a surge of power beginning to swell inside his chest. The energy coursed through his body, reaching every limb to the point where he felt he might explode.

Suddenly the sapphire went dark. The leaf lock snapped open, falling away from the book, and Sam felt a gush of emptiness sweep over his body as the energy left him. It was like he was a balloon and someone had just let all the air out of him.

He sat motionless, holding the book before him. His hands were still trembling, but the tingling sensation had passed. He looked down at the open lock that now hung loosely from the book. Carefully, Sam opened the ivy clasp and slid the book free.

Butterflies ricocheted around in his stomach, and his heart pounded so hard against his chest that he could see his hand twitching. He wasn't sure if he was supposed to see what was inside this book but he had to know more. He took the golden leaf that protected the corner and tried to open the book.

Sam soon realized that the book wasn't a book at all, but rather a storage box of some kind. He lifted the lid of the unusual box and looked inside. It was lined in black velvet and smelled of lavender. Inside were several items: a silver ring, a photograph, a small scroll of parchment, and a leather pouch.

He picked up the ring and held it in his hand. It was large, heavy, and would definitely not fit the finger of anyone in his family. He examined it carefully; there was a ruby red jewel in the center of a star that was surrounded by a thin circle. Four smaller elemental symbols were engraved around the ring. *First the mirror in the cave, then the book, and now the ring—all with the same element signs.* Fear crept through Sam as he worked through the similarities. There were too many coincidences; they had to be linked somehow. But how?

How did the book get here? Did the stranger outside his window put it in the garage, or was he looking for it? Why were the elemental symbols on the mirror and the box and the ring? Sam sat on the floor, staring at the ring. Finally, he placed it back in the box and removed the photo.

It was a black-and-white picture of a small cottage with a lamp post in the center of the yard. There was a small sign that hung from the post but he couldn't make out what it said. It looked like a nice place; peaceful, he thought.

Sam placed the picture back in the box and removed the pouch. It was made of black leather with a gold drawstring. It was heavy and from the sound it made as Sam picked it up, there was something inside.

Sam set the box on the floor and held the pouch in one hand. With the other he gently pulled on the pouch until it opened. Slowly, he emptied out some of the contents into his hand. A few black, triangular crystals slid out. They were thin and about six inches in length. They looked like they were made of Onyx; he could tell because of the thin gray swirls that ran throughout them. Sam would recognize Onyx anywhere; it was his father's birthstone. He took out the rest of the crystals from the pouch and counted them. There were eleven in all.

He looked back into the box to see if he was missing one but he wasn't. *That's strange,* he thought, *why eleven?* He was expecting an even number. Most things came in pairs, but perhaps one had been lost, or maybe they could be used individually, whatever they did.

Sam placed the crystals back into the pouch and put it back into the box. Next he took out the scroll of parchment. He pulled on the small blue ribbon that held the scroll tight. The paper loosened as the ribbon fell back into the box. It was old and felt thick to the touch. He gently took the edge of the scroll and unrolled it with both hands.

Sam could see it was a hand-written letter. To his surprise, it was addressed to his mother.

He looked back at the box and then back at the letter.

His skin began to prickle with sudden awareness. *This is Mom's box, not the stranger's.*

Why in the world would his mother be hiding this in the first place? What made this box and its contents so important that she felt the need to keep it a secret? What was she afraid of? Sam looked back down at the letter, and began to read it.

Dear Alisa,

I was just thinking of you and how much fun we had in Mr. Dolen's class the other day! I don't think I have ever laughed so hard in my life. Who would have known that you could screw up a Calling test so badly. You had Mr. Dolen screaming and running around like crazy. To be honest, I didn't know he could move that fast. That's what I love about you Alisa—you are always good for a laugh.

Anyway, I will miss you over winter break. Have fun meeting Rylan's parents—I know they'll love you! Write me when you can!

Love you!
Holly
P.S.
Just in case you want to practice the Calling again, remember, Narravista.

Sam read and reread the letter, trying to make sense of it. It must have been from an old classmate of hers when she was a kid.

None of this made any sense; this was just a letter from a school friend, so why hide it?

The questions were staring to pile up and things were becoming more complicated. There were disappearing people outside Sam's house, and now there was magic everywhere he turned. He knew he was getting in over his head and it was time to tell his mother.

He would never forgive himself if the stranger harmed someone in his family. Whoever or whatever was lurking outside was a threat; that much he had decided. Why else would this person be spying on him? This time, he would have to make his mother listen. Besides, she had some explaining of her own to do. She was the one who had told him to clean the garage, and she had hidden this box from him and Sarah. After all, it's not like he went looking for it. He found it doing what she asked him to do in the first place, and now she would have to explain the box, and the magic behind it.

Sam looked back down at the scroll and focused on the sentence about the Calling. *What is a Calling?* he wondered. *And what does Narravista mean?*

"Nar-ra-vista," he said slowly, trying to sound the word out.

"Narravista!" he said again more quickly.

Suddenly a large crash rang out over head. Sam lunged forward, thinking the ceiling was caving in. But it wasn't. He turned quickly to see the baseball that he had tossed into a paint bucket earlier spinning near the ceiling.

Sam's mouth fell open; he dropped the letter and spun around to take a better look. The ball went flying to the left side of the garage, slamming into the wall and splintering the wood on impact. It was spinning so fast that wisps of smoke began to appear from the friction against the wall.

Sam fell back on the floor in shock. The baseball shot to the ground slamming into the floor and back to the ceiling above him.

Just then, Travis rounded the corner of the garage, smiling. "Well, it looks like someone's been busy," he said, looking around at the clean garage.

"Travis, look out!" Sam yelled.

Travis looked over just in time to see the speeding baseball heading toward him.

"Holy crap!"

He fell to the ground as the ball shot past him like a missile, missing him by inches.

The ball blasted through the stacked boxes, sending clothes flying into the air. Then it shot out of the garage, up to the roof of the house, and back toward the ground.

"What in the world was that?" Travis yelled.

"I don't know! I don't know what's happening!" Sam said as he rolled over onto his stomach trying to get up.

Without warning the ball came crashing down through the ceiling of the garage. Wood and shingles fell from the roof around Sam. The ball bounced on the floor and shot through the lawn chair, ricocheting back toward Travis.

Travis rolled right dodging the baseball as it pierced another stack of boxes, sending Legos and Barbie body parts in all directions.

"How can we stop it?" Travis asked, rolling into a corner of the garage.

"I don't know! Sam yelled, turning onto his back to get up again.

The ball exploded through the roof once more, sending

the bikes that were hanging on hooks crashing down on Sam's legs. Sam quickly covered his face as debris rained down around him. A large wooden beam from the roof had pinned the bikes on top of him.

Travis quickly got to his feet and pressed his back to the wall, avoiding the spinning baseball at all costs.

"Sam!" he called out. "Don't move! It's right by you!"

Sam lay there frozen; he could hear the hum of the baseball cutting through the air as it spun directly above him. Seconds passed before he felt brave enough to peek through his hands and look at the spinning baseball, hovering just inches above his face.

He could feel the cool breeze wafting off the spinning ball and smell the leather in the air. The ball was moving so fast that the red stitching had become a blur. Sam was scared to move, not knowing what the ball would do next. His foot was stuck in the spokes of the bike and beads of sweat were trailing down the side of face.

Unsure what to do, Sam moved as quickly as he could by placing his hands at his sides and trying to roll to the right, but it was no use. He was pinned down. The ball shot toward the far side of garage and collided into the tools hanging on the wall. Clanking and clattering rang out as the tools came crashing down on the concrete floor.

"Sam!" Travis said. "Are you all right?"

Sam tried to move his legs again but they wouldn't budge under the weight of the beam and the bikes. He was stuck but it didn't feel like he was injured.

"Yeah, I think so, but my legs are stuck!" he said.

Travis paused and watched the spinning baseball eat

away at the wall as Sam flailed under the weight of the bikes. When he rolled right, the ball moved right. As Sam reached for the bikes and tried to move them off his legs, the ball flew to floor in front of him. Sam reacted by flinging himself back down on the floor and as he did the ball flew back to the right of the garage and slammed into the wall again.

Travis watched intently, his eyes scrutinizing every move Sam made. He didn't notice it at first because he assumed the ball was trying to attack Sam. All his attention had been focused on the flying ball. But now that he was watching Sam he could tell the ball wasn't trying to attack him—it was following him. The ball was reacting to Sam's movements. Sam was controlling the ball!

"Sam!" Travis yelled out. "I think the ball is following you!"

"What? What do you mean?" Sam asked.

"It's following you! Maybe your hands, I'm just not sure which one!"

Sam moved his left hand but nothing happened. The ball stayed still, spinning on the wall.

"Sam, try your right hand!" Travis said, crouching down into the corner.

Sam swung his right hand around to the back of the garage and the ball followed, shooting through the air until it hit the back wall of the garage.

Sam's mind was racing. If he could control it, surely he could stop it.

He slowly moved his hand in front of him, as if to guide the ball into the center of the garage. The spinning baseball followed. It was now hovering just a few feet in front of him.

Sam stared at the baseball, trying to concentrate; maybe it was as simple as saying stop, he thought.

"STOP!" he yelled out.

But nothing happened. The ball continued to spin.

"Um, now what?" Travis said hastily.

"I'm not sure!" Sam replied.

"Try something else, like halt or land!"

Sam thought of the letter. *If the word Narravista made this happen, maybe it will make it stop too.*

"Narravista!" Sam yelled out.

The ball abruptly stopped spinning and fell to the ground.

"That's it, you did it!" Travis cried out.

He sprang up, ran to Sam's side and carefully helped to remove the wooden beam and bikes that had fallen on top of Sam. Sam moaned as he staggered to his feet.

"Are you okay?" Travis asked.

Sam brushed himself off and surveyed the damage around him. The garage had two gaping holes in the roof and splintered wood on both sides of the walls. The lawn chair, the bikes, and all the boxes he had packed and stacked earlier were destroyed.

"Yeah, yeah, I'm okay," he said grudgingly, "but my mom's going to kill me!"

"Sam, what happened? I mean, you were controlling that baseball, you were making it fly! It was like you were us-ing—" Travis voice stopped abruptly. He didn't want to say it; the word scared him now, but what else could it be?

"Magic," Sam said calmly.

He saw the look on Travis face; it was that same look he'd had back in the cave. The look of anxiety and bewilderment all rolled into one.

"Yeah, magic," Travis said reluctantly.

Sam could tell it was the last word he wanted to use, but what else could you call it? He needed to make sense of this, he had to or he was going to lose his mind.

"I think it has to do something with the box I found in the wall."

"In the wall? What box? Where?" Travis asked. Now he was curious.

Sam pointed to the back of the garage at the box next to the open panel in the wall.

"How did that get there?" Travis asked.

"I think it's my mom's," he said.

Travis turned around, his eyes wide and his mouth half open in disbelief. "Your mom's?"

"Yeah, in the box there was a letter addressed to her from someone named Holly."

"Who's Holly?"

"Well, if I knew that I wouldn't have said 'someone named Holly,'" Sam said sharply.

"Oh, yeah, right," Travis said as he walked toward the box. "Is it safe to pick it up?"

"Yeah, I think so. I don't think the box did anything. I think it's more what the letter says that makes things happen."

"What do you mean?" Travis asked.

"Read the letter," Sam said pointing to the box.

Travis bent down and grabbed the letter and began to read it to himself. Sam continued to look in disbelief at the damage a baseball could do to a garage.

When he finished reading, Travis looked up from the letter with a puzzled look in his eyes.

"What is Narra—"

"Don't say it!" Sam yelled out! "Are you crazy? You want to get us killed!"

"That's the word you used to stop it!" Travis said defiantly.

"Yeah, and it's also the word I used to make it happen in the first place, so don't say it!"

Travis looked back down at the letter and then at the box. He slowly bent down and picked up the pouch.

"What's in here?" he asked.

Sam shrugged. "Don't know, take a look."

Travis opened the pouch and pulled out one of the slivers of black onyx.

"Wow, that's pretty cool."

He touched the tip of the long triangle.

"Man, that would hurt if you fell on it. Looks like there's quite a few of these things too," Travis said.

"Eleven," Sam replied.

"Weird. Odd number ..."

"Everything is odd about that box," Sam sighed. "There's some kind of picture in there too, but I don't know what it is."

Travis put the crystals back into the pouch and placed it back in the box. He glanced at the picture, but it was the ring that caught Travis's attention.

"Whose ring is this?" he asked, holding it up.

Sam moved closer, stepping over the wooden beams and around the bikes. "I'm not sure," he said.

Travis brought the ring closer to his face to take a better look. He examined it carefully, scrutinizing every detail. Then he stopped and gazed up at Sam. "There's something written on the inside," he said.

Sam met his gaze. "What? How did I miss that? What does it say?"

Travis looked back down at the ring and swallowed, then spoke with a slight hesitation, knowing that what he was about to say was going to hurt.

"It says: Rylan, a Keeper of faith."

Travis looked up at Sam. His cheeks were flushed and he had a solemn blank stare on his face. The words hung in the air and for a brief moment there was silence.

"My father?" Sam said in a broken whisper.

Sam hadn't spoken of his father much, but Travis knew how he felt about him. Travis felt the same way about his parents. Just because you didn't speak about them didn't mean you weren't thinking about them.

He handed the ring over to Sam and purposely began sifting through the scattered remains of the garage, trying to busy himself and give Sam a moment.

Just then, the back door sprang open and Sarah marched onto the porch. Her cell phone was to her ear in one hand and the other was waving in the air. Sam jumped in surprise and quickly shoved the ring into his pocket.

"That's fine Barry. FINE! But if you didn't want to date me any more, all you had to do was man up and say so! You didn't have to cheat on me, you CREEP!"

Sarah began pacing back and forth.

"Scared!" she yelled. "I'm not scared of being alone! The only thing that scares me is that someone might hate me as much as I loathe you. And just for the record, you're not as cool as you think you are! I hate that stupid football jersey you always wear, and you're dumb, and there is no cure for that, Barry!"

Sarah pulled the phone from her ear, and pressed the End button with so much force Sam thought she might snap the phone in half.

"What a loser!"

Sam and Travis stood there in silence. Sam still clutched the ring in his pocket. He rocked back and forth, hoping Sarah would be too flustered to see the wreckage they were standing in.

Sam looked over at Travis, who stood staring at Sarah with a devilish grin. There was a small part of Travis that actually enjoyed seeing that. Maybe not the fact that she was hurt, but the fact that there was no more Barry in her life.

Sam was trying to get Travis's attention when he finally snapped out of his trance. He quickly took to surveying the area once more as if he had heard nothing.

Sarah shoved her cell phone into her pocket and turned to walk back inside when suddenly she stopped. Slowly, she turned her head and her mouth fell open as she looked over the strung out contents of the garage.

"What in the world did you do, Sam?" she asked, flabbergasted.

Sam stood dumfounded, his mind searching for the perfect explanation.

"I ... um ..."

"Um, what, Sam?" she said. "It looks like the garage threw up on you! Mom is going to kill you!"

"Yeah, but ... you see ..."

"Uh, yeah, I do see. I see that you're going to be grounded for the rest of your life if you don't clean up this mess before Mom gets home!"

Sarah shook her head, turned, and walked back into the house. "Men—they can't do anything right!" Sam heard her say to herself.

He stood staring at the back door as it slammed shut and the familiar feeling of utter failure crept back over him.

Nothing ever works out as it should, he thought. *Nothing!*

He reached into his pocket and pulled out his dad's ring. He stared at it for a moment before walking over to the porch steps and sitting down.

The red ruby glistened in the sun as he moved it around in his fingers. The inscription was rough to the touch as he ran his finger around the inner band.

"You know, I never even met him," Sam said softly. "My father, I mean. How can you miss a person you've never even met?" He sighed. "I guess that sounds pretty pathetic, huh?"

Travis turned, walked over to Sam, and sat down next to him on the porch. He brought his legs to his chest and placed his chin on his knees.

"It's not pathetic, Sam," he said.

"Oh, isn't it?" Sam said, staring at the ring.

"No, but maybe it's a wanting feeling, more than a missing one, and there is nothing pathetic about wanting things to be different."

Sam brushed away a tear that began to fall down his cheek and cleared his voice, trying to keep his composure.

"There is just so much about him that I don't know. I mean, my mother never goes into any great detail; we barely talk about him. And now I find this hidden box with *his* ring and a letter from *her* past. And let's not forget the magic spell, or whatever the heck that was. It's like the older I get, the more questions I have and nobody wants to talk about it.

"Sometimes when I'm with my mom it feels like the whole room is filled up with everything we don't say to one another. It's like I don't know who we are—like there's some kind of big secret and I'm the only one that's not in on it."

Travis turned and looked over at Sam. "I'm not sure what your mother is thinking, but whatever it is, Sam, I'm sure she has her reasons. She loves you—she loves you and Sarah, and she's trying so hard to take care of you. It can't be easy on her either, and what's worse is she did know your dad. She loved him for years and then he was gone. Imagine that pain. Maybe she doesn't want to relive that—maybe it just hurts too much."

Sam could hear the pain in Travis's voice. He wasn't sure if Travis was still talking about Sam's mother or his own family. Either way, he knew what it was like to want something you could never have again.

Both Sam and Travis sat for a few moments longer, staring into the garage, thinking about nothing and everything all at once.

The sun had moved behind the house by the time they began to straighten up the garage once more. The hours passed quickly with two people working on the mess and before Sam knew it, he was done again.

There was more trash on the curb than before and less stuff in the garage. The holes in the roof of the garage were patched with leftover particle board they had found in the corner. It would probably leak, but it was the best they could do for now.

Travis helped Sam carry the last of the garbage to the curb. The pile was huge; it looked like the Dalcomes were moving. Barron had already made his way from across the street to investigate the foreign rubbish.

The boys walked back up the driveway to the garage and Sam reached down and picked up his mother's box from the ground. He had already placed all the items back in the box and sealed the lock.

"So what now? Are you going to say something to your mom?" Travis asked.

Sam was so frustrated. He was struggling between what he wanted to know, and what he needed to know.

"I'm not sure I have a choice, Travis. I need to know what's happening and she obviously knows something about all this. And maybe she knows something about the stranger too."

Chapter 5

Gordon Delcour stood watch in the narrow passageway of the cavern. He had removed the ridiculous Earth attire he had been wearing and placed the pants, shirt, and long coat at the mouth of the cave. Now he was fully dressed in his Keeper scout attire. The black body suit felt snug and secure, like a second skin. The weight of the light armor felt familiar, just the way he liked it.

He had only been on Earth for a few days but he was absolutely sure he didn't like it. It was hot and the land was flat—unlike Haven with its rolling hills, endless streams, lakes, and mountain views. Gordon missed those views, but most of all he missed the ocean. He didn't know how Alisa Dalcome had stayed hidden here for so long. But perhaps if traveling to Earth was the only way to protect his children, then maybe he would have done the same.

Gordon knelt down and lit a trail of Kamber Stones throughout the entrance of the cavern. He took a stone and rubbed it in the palm of his hand until it gave off a diminutive green glow. The friction from his hand would keep the stones illuminated for hours.

Now that Holly had arrived, Gordon was instructed by Xavier to guard the cavern and wait for reinforcements. He had spent most of the morning keeping a watch on the back of the house while Holly protected the front and Xavier followed Alisa to work. When evening rolled around, Xavier had sent a scroll ordering Gordon to return to the cavern. Alisa would be returning home soon, and together Holly and Xavier would look after the Dalcomes and try to keep them safe. Once the reinforcements arrived they would be divided into two groups, one to protect the Dalcomes, and the other to search for any traces of the alleged Viper.

Gordon had never seen a Viper before; most people hadn't in real life. Vipers were dark mystical creatures conjured from the spirit world, soulless banshees with the ability to transform from a corporeal being to a non-corporeal being at will. It was said that only the strongest magic could kill them, magic that was rumored to have died out centuries ago. Vipers had only one known weakness—they must feed on the living to walk amongst the living. Starvation was the quickest way to kill a Viper. It was the way they had been killed in the breeding camps back in the Great War, and it would most likely be the way they would have to be killed again.

The notion of hunting a Viper made Gordon's skin crawl. It was one thing to fight an adversary head on, but to fight something that attacks from the shadows with such ferocity you don't even have time to scream before you die? Well, that was different. There was a reason why there were no accurate descriptions of a Viper. No one had ever lived to talk about it.

Still, Gordon had not spent years of hard work at the Academy just to wait around in a cave. He wanted to be where the real action was. He wanted to be with Xavier as he had been the day before. Of course, he wasn't as experienced as Holly, and yes, he was young, fresh out of the Academy. But he had graduated top of his class and now all he was doing was guarding rocks. Gordon jabbed at the gravel with the end of his staff.

When he had heard that the Minister of Justice had requested him to work with Xavier Ward, one of the Majesty's Master Keepers, second only to Demetrius Lore, for a top secret mission, Gordon had been elated. The days of standing guard on Haven waiting for a real mission were over, he hoped. He was ready now, ready to do what he had been trained to do—to serve and protect, to be the Keeper of the Faith. It didn't get any better than that.

But instead, here he was again, doing what he always did, which was nothing. Being stuck in some dreary cave listening to himself breathe was not his idea of action. It was more like dying a slow death.

The Viper probably wasn't even there, and if it was, it would be after the Dalcomes, not hanging around underground somewhere.

Gordon looked down at the triangular gem poised on the hilt of his staff, Alek. The gem began to give off a purple glow, signaling that he was receiving an incoming scroll. He held Alek firmly in one hand and quickly tapped the tip of the gem with the other. A purple flame burst from the end of the staff, engulfing the gem in light. At the center of the fire was a floating scroll of parchment. Gordon quickly reached into the fire and snatched the scroll. The fire was cool to the touch, but that mostly depended on Alek's mood. He shook open the letter and began to read,

Nightfall is upon us, keep a watchful eye.
Be safe.
Xavier

Gordon rolled his eyes. "Yes, sir," he hissed as he watched the scroll slowly dissolve in his hand. The flame on his staff went out and the only light remaining was the soft green glow of the Kamber Stones.

He began to move down the passageway toward the entrance. He needed some air. Besides, it would be dark soon, which meant he was less likely to be seen now by the average person passing by. But to be on the safe side, Gordon thought, it might be wise to bring the jacket.

He walked toward the entrance and saw the Earth garments still sitting where he had left them. As he approached he heard the faint sound of someone crying.

Gordon froze in his tracks and listened intently. He could hear the soft cries of what sounded like a small child from behind him. But how could that be? No one had come in. If they had, he would have seen them. He was sure of that.

Gordon strained his eyes, looking back into the darkness. There was nothing there but the winding passageway, dimly lit by the glowing green stones.

He turned to face the cave, his boots grinding the gravel beneath him. In the distance, coming from somewhere beyond the end of the passageway, he heard it again. But this time it spoke.

"Help me, please."

Startled, Gordon raised Alek in front of him. The staff, sensing his fear, began to shine, casting a purple glow on the scene before him.

"Hello, who's there?" he asked.

Gordon listened for a reply, but there was no answer.

"Hello?" he said again. "Is someone there?"

He heard footsteps running on the gravel ground just beyond his line of sight but it was too dark to see anything clearly.

"Who's there?" he said. He could not hide the anxiety in his voice.

"Help me!" the voice said. It was the voice of a young girl.

Quickly, Gordon moved his right hand in a circular motion around the gemstone of his staff. Thin strands of light peeled away from the gem, gathering in Gordon's hand. The strands spun together until they formed a brilliant ball of light the size of his palm.

Gordon pulled his hand back and gently pushed the ball of light down the tunnel. He watched as it travelled the length of the passageway. Off in the distance he could still hear the whimpering child. The light reached the first bend in the passageway and then he saw her. Her back was facing him; she wore a torn, filthy white dress, and no shoes. She had brown shoulder-length hair that was matted in thick strands and her arms and legs were covered in cuts, scrapes, and bruises. In her left hand she held a stuffed pink rabbit by the ears.

The sphere of light began to fade as it finally reached the little girl. The passageway grew dim once again, and the small child inched away around the corner. Gordon could hear her little feet padding on the gravel.

"No! Wait!" Gordon said. "Come back!"

He began to run down the winding path, in hopes of reaching the child before she got to the cavern. The Kamber Stones were not bright enough to illuminate the entire cavern and it would be dangerous for her to enter with the stalagmites protruding from the ground.

Gordon reached the end of the tunnel, but the little girl was nowhere to be found. Alek shone brighter as Gordon advanced into the cavern. As he held up his staff, he could barely make out the floating portal in the distance. A large body of water stood between him and the portal, taking up most of the cavern.

Gordon felt a cool refreshing breeze move across his skin, but something felt wrong. She should be there. Just then, Alek began to vibrate beneath his grip. Gordon grasped his staff tightly and moved it to the right, slowly searching for the child. The light fell across the water which looked like glass, silent and motionless.

"Hello, are you there?" Gordon asked, swallowing hard. But still there was no reply.

He moved the staff back to the right, its purple glare reaching the far depths of the cavern, but again he saw no sign of the girl.

"Where are you?" he asked again. "I won't harm you. I'm here to help you."

"Help," the voice said again. This time it was coming

from the center of the cavern. Gordon quickly moved Alek around to take a better look. There, sitting in the shallow water in front of the floating portal, was the small child. She was kneeling with her face in her hands and the rabbit floated next to her in the water.

How did she get out there? Gordon wondered. She hadn't been there a minute ago.

She was crying now, her body trembled with every sob. She was obviously frightened, Gordon thought. "Please ... help me," she said again. Her voice was softer this time, almost a whisper.

Taking a deep breath, Gordon walked with a sense of purpose past the stalagmite-infested shoreline and down into the body of water. He waded through the water with Alek held firmly in front of him, guiding the way. The staff was vibrating fiercely in his hand, but Gordon ignored the warning. All he could think about was the child and that she needed his help. Maybe Alek is sensing the child's fear, he guessed.

"I'm coming, don't be scared. I'll be right there."

As Gordon approached the child's body cringed in terror. She reached for the floating rabbit and pulled it close to her.

Gordon stared down at the girl. The skin on her arms was ashen white, and upon closer inspection he could see that she had several deep gashes on her arms, some shallow scrapes, and her hands were bleeding.

Good Lord, what's happened to this girl?

He moved closer to comfort her. She was sobbing into her hands and clutching the rabbit.

"It's okay, I'm here. Everything is going to be all right," he said.

As Gordon shifted Alek around to better see the child, he noticed a black mass moving over the child's legs in the water. Quickly, he brought Alek close, and what he saw made his stomach turn.

Hundreds of black spiders were swarming over the girl's legs and moving up her dress onto her waist. Gordon reached down for her.

"Come quickly, there are spiders—" but before he could finish his sentence the child reached out and snatched his arm with such force that he winced in pain. Sharp, bone-gray nails dug into his flesh. Shocked, Gordon looked up at the child, and for the first time, he saw her grotesque face.

Red glowing pupils surrounded by milky white irises stared intently back at him. Streaky black veins riddled the child's face. Her emaciated eye sockets were tinged with black and her thin cracked lips were pallid and bloodstained.

Gordon fell to his knees with a splash; the pain in his arm was so excruciating he found it almost impossible to move. Alek's vibrations intensified and the purple gemstone surged with an intense brilliance.

Gordon tried his best to focus, Calling on the element of Water. His connection with the element was weak, but from the corner of his eye he could see the water swirling on either side of him to form long, spinning funnels. He could use the water to suffocate the creature, if only he could maintain the connection long enough.

The child sneered, her eyes rolling back into her head until only the whites of her eyes were visible. She opened her mouth, revealing several rows of long, serrated teeth.

Gordon struggled desperately, trying to pull himself

free, but she was too strong. Her grip tightened, nails digging into Gordon's flesh so deeply that they punctured the muscle and scraped the bone. The creature let out a blood-curdling scream as it pulled him closer.

With deadly precision the Viper struck Gordon's neck, tearing into his flesh. The Calling of the Water he had conjured only moments ago began to dissolve, and Gordon felt himself go weak.

It was at that moment Gordon Delcour knew he was going to die, and that he would do so at the hands of the monster they called the Viper. His body went limp, and Alek fell from his dying grasp into the bloodstained water.

CHAPTER 6

The sun was setting when Travis and Sam finally made their way back inside and up to Sam's room. They didn't see any sign of Sarah, which meant she was avoiding them. *That's actually a good thing,* Sam thought. If Barry had really broken up with his sister, she was probably in her room mending her ego. After all, no one ever broke up with the Queen of Mean, much less cheat on her. Sam almost felt sorry for Bone Head Barry, but then he thought better of it.

"Wow, you weren't joking. Your room is clean. You feeling all right?" Travis asked, his wide eyes surveying the room.

Sam ignored the sarcasm; he was more interested in a rather large detail that seemed to have escaped him with all the chaos in the garage. Travis looked different. His bangs weren't hanging in his eyes like normal. Now they were combed back and his hair was parted neatly to one side. His clothes were different too—they didn't involve the color orange.

"Travis," Sam said, amused.

"Yeah?"

"So, what's up with the hair and the new clothes?"

"What?" Travis asked. "That's crazy talk." He looked away, pretending to be interested in how clean the room looked.

"Really. I've known you forever ... well, like almost forever and I think I would know if you looked different."

Travis's cheeks began to flush and he still would not look directly at Sam.

"I don't know what you're talking about," he replied. His tone was calm but everything else screamed *I'm so busted!* "Don't you have a shower to get in?"

Sam couldn't help but grin. He knew what this was about—it was about Sarah. She had actually been nice to Travis the other day for the first time in his life and that had given him hope. A fool's hope, but Travis wasn't going to give up on her no matter how uninterested she seemed. His subtle persistence wouldn't get him far, however. If there was one thing Sam knew for sure, it was that girls like Sarah didn't date guys like Travis. Sarah had said something similar herself when other, less attractive guys had asked her out.

"Beauty never really dated the beast; that's something ugly people say to make themselves feel better," she had said. His sister was pretty much a cold-hearted man-eater, and she wouldn't think twice about casting your ego and soul into Siberia. If Travis didn't watch it, his would end up there too.

Travis looked over at Sam inconspicuously, not sure if he believed him or not. Sam didn't say another word; he had tried to reason with Travis in the past, regarding his sister.

But Travis didn't get it or he didn't care, Sam wasn't sure which. But he did know the Queen of Mean needed her minions, and if Travis wanted to wait in that line, so be it.

Sam turned and gathered his things and headed into the bathroom to take a shower. He was still covered in dirt after having dealt with the garage. Once Sam had closed the bathroom door Travis sat aimlessly on his bed, staring at the collage of dragon posters on the wall. He wasn't quite sure how Sam managed to get any sleep at night with these creatures staring down at him like that. They were scary, not to mention some were just flat out weird. There were dragons of every shape, size and color; some had thick, long serpentine bodies covered in a scaly skin. Others looked more like reptiles or lizards with massive bat-like wings, wedge-shaped heads, and long, tapered necks. They all had powerful legs, ending with sharp talons or claws. Some were fire breathers, others ice breathers.

Travis continued to stare, lost in the sea of magnificent colors, when he heard what sounded like a faint moan coming from the hallway. He turned his head slowly, waiting to hear it again.

Again the soft moan came from somewhere beyond Sam's door. At first Travis thought Barron had gotten into the house again. But after hearing it a third time, it sounded more like a person than an animal. He got up from the bed and tiptoed to the edge of Sam's bedroom door. The whimpering became louder and for a moment it almost sounded like someone was crying. Travis peeked out around the door, looking both ways down the hallway. There was no one in sight, but the sounds seemed to be coming from Sarah's room.

Travis moved quietly down the hall, stopping just inches away from Sarah's closed door. His heart was beating so loudly against his chest it sounded like he was knocking on her door already. Travis had never been this close to Sarah's room before. He had always steered clear of it, knowing that she would probably kill him if he got too close. Hoping no one would come down the hallway, and that Sarah wouldn't open the door, he moved a bit closer. He could just imagine that conversation.

"Hi Sarah. Oh, what am I doing standing by your door, you ask? Why, I'm stalking you, of course."

That would not be good. It was bad enough that Sarah hated him but to be her stalker too, well that was a bit much, even for him.

Against his better judgment, Travis inched closer, placing his ear on the door. He stared down at the bedroom light seeping into the hallway from beneath the door. He could hear faint whimpers and sniffling. He had never heard Sarah cry before. In fact, in all the time he had known her, Travis had never seen any emotion, other than pure annoyance, from Sarah. But maybe that was because he was Travis and she was Sarah.

He couldn't imagine what on Earth could make Sarah cry like this; she was the toughest girl he knew. She had the perfect life—everyone loved her, guys wanted to date her and girls wanted to be her. Nothing about this made any sense.

The crying became softer. She was mumbling something between her sobs but he couldn't make it out. He strained to hear more and pressed his ear against the door. He heard something about Barry being such a jerk. Not realizing the door was not properly latched, he pressed his ear harder against the door and fell right into the room.

A loud thud rang out as Travis's face slammed into the wooden floor. Sarah let out a high-pitched squeal and jumped back against her headboard.

"Travis, what are you doing?" she yelled.

He flopped around in panic, trying desperately to regain his composure. But there was no hiding the fact that he looked like an overturned turtle trying to right himself.

"I'm sorry, Sarah, I'm sooo sorry!" he said as he got to his knees and looked up at Sarah's horror-stricken face.

"TRAVIS. WHAT. ARE. YOU. DOING!" she yelled again.

Travis's mouth fell open, flabbergasted, as the events of the past few minutes flooded over him. She was fuming and she had every right to be. He had invaded her privacy. He got to his feet, his hands out stretched as he tried to plead his case.

"Sarah, please I am so sorry ... I heard you crying from the hallway ... I thought something was wrong!"

Sarah glared at Travis from her bed. Her knees were pulled close to her body and she gripped her pillow in one hand and her cell phone in the other, as if she was ready throw them at any minute.

"You were eavesdropping on me, Travis, in my own house!"

Travis's mouth was still open but nothing was coming out. This was not going well at all.

"No ... no that's not it at all, you were crying, you see, you were upset. I ... just wanted to make sure you were okay?"

"Well, how do you think I'm doing now?" she asked, still furious.

Travis was again caught off guard, "Well ... I ... um ..."

"I'm not good Travis, NOT GOOD!" she yelled. "You had no right. This is my personal business, NOT yours! Do you understand that? CAN you understand that?"

Travis lowered his head. This had all gone horribly wrong. He had never meant to eavesdrop; he just wanted to make sure she was okay.

"Sarah, I'm sorry. I didn't mean to, I just ..." He struggled with the words. "I care about you," he said finally in frustration. The words were out before he even realized it.

The room fell silent as they both stared at one another. Travis swallowed nervously. He didn't know whether to run, apologize again, or just keep his mouth shut. Sarah's furrowed eyebrows softened and her mouth fell open. They continued to look at one another in silence until Sarah finally closed her mouth and cleared her throat.

Travis debated throwing himself out of the window. How in the world had he let that come flying out of his mouth? He could feel himself blushing, but he wasn't the only one. Sarah was turning red too. There was an uncomfortable air between the two of them now. They awkwardly glanced around the room, looking anywhere but at each other.

After a long silence, Travis finally turned to leave the room, completely mortified. This was the final straw, he was sure of that. He felt like an epic idiot. He couldn't even count the times he had made a fool out of himself in front of Sarah—there were too many. But today was without a doubt the most appalling display of stupidity he had ever conjured up in a single moment. Even he was impressed at how lame he could be.

He looked back at Sarah with his sad brown eyes "I'm sorry ..." he whispered. He turned away with his head hung low and gradually walked back through the doorway.

"Travis ... wait," Sarah said softly.

Travis stopped and looked over his shoulder.

"It's ... okay." she said, hesitantly. "I mean, it's not okay, but I know you meant well." The right side of her lip curled up slowly in a half grin. "You always mean well, I guess. I was just a little freaked out, you know?"

Travis nodded, unsure of how to respond. He had never really had a conversation with Sarah before.

"It's just been a really bad day," she said. Her words were sincere and Travis could tell she actually meant what she was saying.

"I would never do anything to hurt you," he said shyly.

"I know ... I've always known that," Sarah replied, looking away.

"Sarah?" Travis asked.

Sarah turned and looked back at Travis. From the look on his face he seemed intimidated, and scared, like a little boy who got caught stealing from the cookie jar.

"If you don't mind me asking, what happened? What's wrong?"

Sarah's eyes slowly filled with tears again.

"It's a long story, Travis, and it's stupid anyway," she said, barely able to get the words out.

"Nothing is ever stupid if it can hurt you," Travis said.

Her gaze softened, as if one of the many walls she had to protect herself had fallen. Travis looked at her. It was odd how much Sam and Sarah were alike. Always guarded, always careful, never letting anyone too close. It was like they were too scared to trust anyone.

"It's Barry," she said, wiping the tear that had fallen down her cheek. "He cheated on me with Mary Fisher last week when I didn't feel like going out."

Travis shook his head in disgust. He had never liked Barry and had always thought of him as a player. He was the typical jock—big head, big ego, and no brains.

"I'm sorry, Sarah. I know you liked him."

Sarah shook her head and straightened herself up on the bed. "That's the thing, Travis, I really didn't. I really didn't like him. I ..." Sarah paused, then looked up at the ceiling, struggling to find the words to convey that she merely put up with Barry.

Travis raised an eyebrow. This was not what he was expecting to hear.

"Then why were you so upset?" Travis asked, confused.

"I was just angry, I guess, more at myself than anything. I mean, I didn't even like the guy and yet I put up with so much of his macho crap. And then he has the nerve to cheat on me! What a giant waste of time!" she said, waving her hands in frustration.

"What a jerk!" Travis chimed in. *This feels good,* he thought. Finally someone other than him and Sam thought that Barry "I Walk On Water" Rogers wasn't so great after all. Travis had to admit it—there was just something about Sarah hating Barry that made him feel all warm and fuzzy inside.

"Yeah!" she said.

"He has a really big head too," Travis continued.

"He does, doesn't he? Wow, I thought I was the only one who thought that," she said, starting to smile.

Travis loved it when she smiled.

"God, he would go on and on about himself. Sometimes I would have my headphones in while he was talking to me, and I would just nod like I knew what he was talking about."

Travis laughed, "Nice!" Sarah laughed too.

"So, why did you stay with him so long?" Travis asked.

It was like someone had slammed on the breaks. Sarah's smile faded and she suddenly became silent again. Her eyes shifted and she looked away. He could tell this was a question she was not sure she wanted to answer.

"It's ... it's okay Sarah, I mean if you don't want to talk about it," he said reassuringly.

She looked back at Travis. She seemed uncomfortable now, almost fragile as she crossed her arms.

"No ... it's okay." Her voice was meek. "He ... he made me feel better about myself," she said. She was ashamed to admit it, but it was true.

Travis was really confused now.

"What, how?" His voice was riddled with aggravation. "Barry was a bully. He was mean to just about every person I know and in the end he wasn't good to you either. So how in the world did he make you feel special?"

"Better," she corrected him. "I said better, not special." She looked back down at her bed.

"I don't understand." Travis could feel the blood rushing

to his face. But it wasn't Sarah he was mad at—it was Barry. It was the fact that this jerk could give Sarah something that he couldn't, something that made her feel better about herself even though he was such a complete jerk. Sarah stared down at the bed, and for a minute Travis didn't think she was going to answer him. Finally, she lifted her head and her eyes were latent with tears.

"Because when I was with him I didn't feel like the worst person in the room. I ..." she wiped a tear from her cheek. "I felt better knowing that there was someone out there worse than me."

Travis felt his heart sink. Sarah looked humiliated. This was a side of her he never knew existed and now that he had seen it, he wished he hadn't. It hurt him somehow to see her in so much pain.

He stood motionless for a moment, looking at the girl he thought he knew. What could he possibly say to that? Travis took a moment before moving from the doorway and walking toward Sarah, who was now staring aimlessly into her pink and white comforter. He stopped and sat down on the bed next to her.

"I never knew you felt like that," he said, looking over at her. Sarah shrugged and pulled her hair behind her ear.

"I know. No one does."

Travis fidgeted with his hands, not knowing what to do with himself.

"You just always seemed, well, like nothing bothered you, like you were okay with everything."

Sarah sighed and looked over at Travis, her light blue eyes meeting his.

"Sometimes, people cry on the inside, Travis," she said, and he could see the pain in her eyes. *How long had she been carrying this around?* he wondered. He nodded and held her gaze.

"Well, you're nothing like Barry, that's for sure," he said.

"I don't know about that," she replied.

Well I do. I know you," Travis said confidently.

"You think you know me," she said.

"No, I do know you."

"No, you don't!" she said in frustration, "Everyone thinks they know me, but they don't! I'm a fake, Travis, and I'm great at hiding it! Did you know that? Huh? Did you know that I despise the girl I see in the mirror every single day because I can't stomach the person I have become, did you know that?"

Travis stared at Sarah, stunned, unable to speak.

"My best friends are liars and backstabbers and I hurt people on a daily basis, and because I've been doing this for so long I don't know who I am anymore!" Her voice finally broke.

"Sarah, stop! That's not true, why would you say that?"

Tears began to stream down her face again and she tried desperately to regain her composure by wiping them away and sitting up straight.

"Because it's true, Travis," she said, catching her breath.

"No, that's not true," he said, trying to reassure her.

"Yes, yes it is. I'm a horrible person, Travis; you know that better than anyone."

This was true; she had never been nice to him. But for Travis, that was okay. It was better than being ignored— that would have been far worse, he thought.

"Well, yeah, but ..."

"But, what?" she continued. She was calming down now.

"But, I never thought you meant it," he said pointedly.

"Oh, and why is that?" she asked, wiping another tear from her face.

"Well ... because I'm man-tastic, and I mean, who doesn't want a piece of this?" he said nudging her with his elbow.

To Travis's delight, Sarah snorted. His remark had caught her by surprise. She quickly covered her mouth, embarrassed, but still couldn't contain her laughter.

Travis began to laugh too. "Hey, why are you laughing? They don't make 'em like this anymore." Sarah laughed harder.

"Hey what's going on?"

It was Sam. He stood in Sarah's doorway in a t-shirt, shorts, and wet hair. He had a bewildered look on his face, as if he had never seen two people laugh before.

Their smiles immediately faded. Both Travis and Sarah stopped laughing, forcing more serious looks onto their faces.

Travis was the first to speak.

"I ... um ... well, I was ..." he rambled.

"He told me a joke," Sarah interrupted.

Sam's face was more puzzled now than ever before. "He did what?"

"A joke. J-O-K-E." she said again, more sarcastically this time.

Now that was the Sarah Sam knew; the laughing a minute ago was a little bizarre.

"Um, yeah, it was just a funny joke," Travis added poorly.

The room was silent again. Everyone stared at each other, wondering who would speak next. Sarah finally spoke.

"Sooo anyway, that was really funny," she said, turning to Travis. "Thanks for telling me that one." Her eyes met his. He smiled and she smiled back. Travis knew she was saying thank you for more than just the joke. He also knew that this would be a day he would never forget.

Chapter 7

It was about eight o'clock when the front door opened and Alisa Dalcome walked into the house. Her beautiful chestnut hair was tied in a loose ponytail and her face seemed pale. She was exhausted after her long day at work. Sam and Sarah were in the kitchen loading the dishwasher while Travis sat idly on the countertop talking to them. They all turned when they heard the door open.

Alisa was dressed in the powder blue diner uniform she affectionately called her "Granny Blues" because of the white ruffled collar and fringe at the bottom. Her purse was draped over her shoulder and she was struggling to keep a hold of the two bags of groceries she was carrying. But as she stepped into the house one of the bags tore, spilling cans, bottles, and small frozen dinner packages onto the floor.

"Ugh, that figures!" she said in an exasperated tone. Shaking her head at the spilt contents, she bent down and began to gather the groceries.

Sam hurried out of the kitchen to help her with Travis close behind.

"We'll get it, Mom!" Sam said, knelling down to gather the groceries.

"Here, let me take that one for you, Mrs. Dalcome," Travis said.

"Thank you, boys, I appreciate it."

Alisa handed Travis the other bag as she closed the door behind her. She stepped around Sam and headed directly to the couch.

"Hey, Mom, wow, you look bad," Sarah said as she walked into the living room, scrutinizing her mother's appearance.

"Thanks, Sarah, I love you too," Alisa said rolling her eyes and plopping herself on the couch.

"I'm kidding, you know I love you," she said smiling over at Travis. "Do you want me to make us some dinner?"

Alisa threw her slender legs on the couch and propped a few pillows behind her head before sighing. "Ah, much better."

"Earth to Mom!" Sarah said.

"What?"

"Dinner?" Sarah repeated.

"Oh, no I brought dinner, it's Chinese night. Travis has it in his bag. I hope you like Kung Pao Chicken, Travis," she said, peering over the top of the couch at him.

"Um, yes, I do, thank you," he replied.

"Good." Alisa said as she disappeared behind the couch again.

Travis grinned and looked over at Sarah. She too was smiling as she took the Chinese food out of the bag. "Oh, I like these green bean things too," Travis said.

Sarah laughed, "Edamame, silly."

"Eda-what?" Travis asked, pulling the carton closer, as if it were a foreign substance.

"Ed-a-ma-me, it's not a green bean; it's a soybean in a pod."

Keeping his eyes on Sarah, Travis pulled one from the container. "Pods, I like those," he said and popped it in his mouth.

Sam had made two trips from the doorway to the kitchen before Travis even remembered that he was there.

"Sorry, Dude, you need any help?" he asked as Sam placed the last can on the counter.

"Um, that would be a no!" Sam said scowling. He wasn't sure what was going on with Travis and Sarah, but whatever it was, it was strange. Sarah was being too nice and it was starting to make Sam uncomfortable. When Sarah was nice, bad things happened, especially to Sam.

"Sooo, how was your day?" Sarah asked her mother.

But again there was no reply.

"Mom?"

"Huh, are talking to me?" Alisa asked. Her eyes were closed now.

"Well, yeah, who else would I be talking to? I know how Sam's day went." Sarah leaned over at Sam and hissed, "I hope you put the garage back together."

Sam's eyes narrowed and his lips pursed. Travis looked at both of them but said nothing.

"Oh, it was fine," Alisa sighed and positioned her head more comfortably on the pillows. "I cured world hunger, but the whole world peace thing is going to take some time."

Travis smiled. It was obvious where Sam and Sarah got their sarcasm.

Sam turned his attention back to his mother; he still needed to apologize for the other night. But he also had some very important questions he needed to ask her. However, she was tired and this was probably not the best time to ask about the storage box, the magic, or the stranger. If Sam was smart, he would apologize first; maybe soften her up a bit before he started in on her secrets.

He made his way around the couch as Travis helped Sarah set the table. Alisa was lying there with her eyes closed and a small grin on her face. He stood for a second, fidgeting with a left over piece of paper he had found in his pocket. This was the moment that he had been dreading. Partly because of the apology, but mostly because of the reaction his mother might have when confronted about the secret box.

Still hesitant, Sam finally sat on the coffee table facing his mother. She looked so peaceful, he thought, even though he knew she was exhausted. She had worked the double shift again, which was always grueling for her. She had gone grocery shopping and even stopped to pick up dinner.

She was a great mother. It was a shame he didn't tell her that more often. He would have to fix that going forward, he thought. Sam cleared his throat, pulled out a piece of paper that had been in his pocket and began to roll it between his finger tips.

"Mom?" he said, almost hoping she wouldn't answer.

Alisa lifted one of her eye lids slightly startled.

"Hey, Sam ..." she said sleepily. Sam's gaze fell from his mother to the floor the moment she looked at him.

"Um, I wanted to talk to you about something." She opened her other eye and turned her head toward Sam.

"Okay ... is everything all right?" Her tone was cautious now, not knowing whether to be worried or not yet.

He began to straighten out the paper with his fingers. He cleared his throat, trying not to sound so nervous.

"Well, yeah I'm okay, but what I wanted to say was about the other night, I'm—"

"Dinner is served, so come and get it!" Sarah said abruptly.

Sam almost jumped out of his skin. He looked up at Sarah with a grimace. Sarah frowned, mouthing the words "What did I do?"

He shook his head and looked back down at his mother, but she was not looking at Sam anymore. She was staring at the small piece of paper in his hand.

"Sam, where did you get that?" she asked. Her tone was serious now.

"What?" Sam asked.

Alisa sat up quickly and grabbed Sam's forearm.

"Sam, where did you get this?" Her voice was loud and he could tell she was frightened.

Sam looked down at the paper, not realizing what he had in his hand. It was the candy wrapper he found in Mrs. Cambridge's front lawn. The candy wrapper that belonged to the stranger.

"I found it outside," he said, feeling her grip tighten on his arm.

"When, Sam? When did you find it?"

"The other day, outside. Why? What's wrong?

Travis and Sarah both turned at the commotion to see Alisa leap from the couch.

"Mom, what's wrong?" Sarah asked, her smile fading.

"They've found us, they know we're here! We're in danger!" Alisa said, clearly frightened.

"Mom, who are you talking about? Are you talking about the man in the coat?" Sam asked, trying to keep up.

Alisa's face turned white. She got up from the couch and headed quickly toward the kitchen.

"Kids, get in the car now!"

Travis looked at Sam; they stared at one another for a moment, knowing that once again they had stumbled onto something bad.

"Mom, why are we leaving? What's going on?" Sarah asked insistently.

Alisa desperately searched the kitchen counter for her car keys. "Where are the keys?" she yelled. She turned to look back at Sam who stood frozen by the couch. His face had gone pale and his eyes were fixed on something above him.

Alisa followed his gaze with her own eyes until she saw what Sam was looking at. Moving from the ceiling down the living room walls were hundreds of black and green spiders, scurrying in a massive swarm toward her son.

"Run, Sam, run!" Alisa yelled.

<h1 style="text-align:center">CHAPTER 8</h1>

Sam ran around the couch and into the kitchen to join the others. His eyes were still trained on the multiplying spiders across the room. He stood in a tight circle with his mother, Travis, and Sarah, watching as the rest of the living room was covered by the swarm of spiders. Thin, black, hairy legs carried the spiders down the walls of the house, onto the floor, and over the couch, until the entire living room was alive with movement.

"Mom, what's happening? Where are they all coming from?" Sarah cried out.

"Everyone stay close!" Alisa shouted back in response.

She turned to open the kitchen door but suddenly stopped when she saw more spiders scurrying between the door and its frame, swarming in from the outside.

The house began to creek and the walls shuddered with the movement of the spiders. Sam watched as deep cracks spread across the kitchen ceiling and small pieces of plaster fell to the floor. The light fixture above them fell loose to one side, exposing several wires. Sarah and Travis jumped away, startled, as sparks rained down. The light flickered on and off like a slow-moving strobe light.

Hundreds of black and green spiders descended from the ceiling cracks on thin, emerald strands of silk. Their tiny legs twitched in rapid succession as their bodies spun in slow circles until they reached the counters and floor.

Everyone stood motionless, watching as the first group of spiders migrated from the living room to the kitchen within seconds. Their long legs tapped the hard wood so fast it seemed like they were gliding across the floor.

The screeching sound they made was all too familiar to Sam and Travis; thoughts of their escape from the cave were still fresh on their minds. Sam would never forget their round bodies with the three green stripes and small circle near their heads. Just the sight of them made him cringe.

The spiders quickly overwhelmed the kitchen, covering the counters and floor in green and black. At first, Sam thought they were moving into the kitchen to attack them, but that was not the case. It looked like the spiders had no interest in them whatsoever. They scurried by, less than an inch in front of where Sam, Travis, Sarah, and Alisa were standing, but never once broke formation. They had one purpose in mind, and that was to gather in the center of the kitchen.

"Back, children! Back!" Alisa shouted as she continued to edge the group against the wall and out of the room, giving the spiders room to maneuver around them.

She glanced to the front door as a means of escape but it too was covered in spiders. The spiders had formed one wide, winding path that lead from the front door to the kitchen. There was no way out. They were trapped.

Sam stood gawking at the large gathering of creatures as they jumped and climbed over one another. It wasn't the mass chaos it looked like, he thought. The spiders were working together within the pile. They were trying to reach a predetermined location. Just looking at them made Sam's stomach turn. Rapidly, the pile grew larger, and within seconds it had transformed into what looked like a small mountain in the kitchen. It must have been at least six feet tall.

"Mom, we have to get out of here!" Sarah shouted. Her voice trembled as she yelled and her hands were shaking violently. Sam glanced over at Sarah; he had never seen her so scared in his life. Her once olive skin was now pallid and pasty with fear, drained of all color.

"I'm with her!" Travis agreed. His skin looked clammy too, but he was calm as he spoke.

"Move over near the fireplace!" Alisa said, pointing in the direction of the living room. Not a single spider remained in the room beyond them; it was as if nothing had ever been there. Sam, Sarah, and Travis moved quickly past the pile of spiders to the fireplace as instructed.

Alisa looked to the living room window and front door again as a possible exit. But this time it wasn't spiders that stopped her, but a tremor in the air. The feeling grew more intense as the tremor became stronger. But there was no mistaking it now—something was definitely blocking the air current around her home.

Frustrated, Alisa cursed herself; it had been too long since she had used the elements. This was something she should have felt early on. The rebounding current could only mean one thing—a Binding spell. Someone, or something, must have cast the spell around the house once they were all together, locking them in and everything else out. There would be no way out now. She would have to hold the spiders off until the spell was broken from the outside.

"I think we have a problem," Travis said, his hand quivering as he pointed to the kitchen.

The large mass of spiders had begun to change shape, becoming flatter and longer, fusing into something much more dense than before. Flashes of white burst from its center, sending narrow bands of light streaming out in every direction.

Alisa stood, bracing herself in front of the children. The light was so intense that she could hardly look at it. Sarah and Travis shielded their eyes and Sam covered his as well, but he made sure to keep one eye on his mother who stood bravely in front of them.

The sound of dying spiders filled the room with a deafening, ear-piercing screech. Sam watched as their bodies twisted and melted together in a morbid self-sacrifice. A black sheen fell upon the mound as the last of the spiders dissolved. Sam's shoulders tightened and his forehead began to sweat. *This is not going to be good,* he thought.

Alisa saw the mound slowly begin to move, sliding, inching its way across the kitchen floor and into the living room toward them. The flashes of light made it difficult for Alisa to see, but she noticed not a single spider remained, only a solid black mass that was ever changing.

Small lumps surfaced randomly around a thin, black membrane. Something was pushing its way out from the inside. Alisa swallowed hard as she saw the likeness of a human skull press and stretch against the horrid cocoon. There was something alive in there and it was trying to get out.

Suddenly, a long arm tore its way free from the black mass, revealing a gloved hand. Alisa's body went numb, and Sarah gasped and covered her mouth. Travis was staring so hard that his eyes appeared damp and overly bright.

"I'm guessing whatever that is won't be happy when it gets out," Travis said, his voice cracking. Sam couldn't speak; he couldn't feel his legs either. But he could feel his heart pounding in his ribcage.

A pair of boots and a man's legs were the next recognizable features to penetrate the cocoon, followed by its waist, chest, and shoulders.

"Mom, what ... what is that?" Sarah whispered. Alisa could feel her daughter trembling as she touched her shoulder. Sarah was beginning to become unhinged. Travis reached over next to the fireplace with one hand and grabbed a shovel from the collection of fireplace tools that hung suspended on a pewter stand. With the other hand he gently pushed Sarah behind him. Sarah looked at Travis and hesitated, unsure what to do.

"I'm not going to let anything hurt you," Travis said. His tone was absolute. She nodded, somewhat shocked, and stepped behind Travis who turned and stood resolute in front of her. Not knowing what to do, Sam did the same and grabbed the poker from the fireplace, holding it out in front of him.

The flashes of light from the cocoon began to dissipate; one by one each stream of light was silenced by the darkness, leaving only the tall ominous figure standing in front of them. The room fell silent except for a slow methodical hiss reverberating from the dark creature.

It was tall and extremely muscular. It had a flat black exoskeleton with overlapping scales that covered its entire body like a snake. Alisa stepped back as the menacing creature stepped forward. Its red reptilian eyes pierced the dark hood that hung like a veil, concealing its face in shadow.

Sarah was the first to react when she saw the creature in its full form. Her shaking hand grabbed Travis's arm.

"That's no spider," she whispered. Her voice was quivering and her eyes were wide and fixed at the bottom of the creature's traveling cloak. It was moving, writhing back and forth in a serpentine motion around its feet as if it were alive.

A hand, the size of a normal man's, firmly gripped a staff. Part of the creature's black glove was torn up to its forearm, revealing sallow skin that was cracked and weathered like rotted wood. Its fingernails were long and stained with blood.

The creature's staff was a twisted, tangled array of human bone and dark wood. The pommel was a single protruding serpent with eyes made of crimson gemstones that flickered in the dim light.

Alisa stared in horror; her heart was racing, adrenaline pumped through her body, and her senses were as alive as they had ever been.

"No," she said, "it ... it can't be."

Sarah's grip tightened around Travis's arm. He was tense but if he was scared he didn't show it in his face. He seemed intent on protecting her and that gave Sarah the courage to speak.

"Mom," she asked softly, "what does it want with us?"

Alisa stared in disbelief at the creature she had helped to eradicate so long ago. Its menacing form was all too familiar from her days of battle in the Great War. But here it was in her home—a Viper, and it was alive.

"Sarah, don't speak. None of you move," Alisa commanded. She took in a deep breath and let it out slowly. *Suppression keeps you calm; calm places you in control,* she thought to herself.

"You will not hurt my children!" she said sharply to the creature in front of her.

The Viper stood motionless, its eyes moving slowly back and forth between her and the children. Its bloodcurdling hiss was once again the only audible sound in the room.

Alisa was running out of time; that much she knew. The Viper was sizing her up and soon it would unleash its dark magic on both her and the children. She could not let that happen, she told herself. She would have to hold it off and buy time for Xavier to break the spell. He was out there and he was trying to save her, she had to believe that. Without that, there was no hope of survival.

Alisa eyed the Viper's flowing black cloak gliding on the floor as if a gentle breeze were blowing it. But there was no breeze; the cloak was alive, and it was just one of the many weapons the Viper had at its disposal.

A low guttural growl resonated from deep within the Viper's throat, then suddenly its blood red eyes locked on Alisa. The cloak quickly fanned out over the floor in two separate strands, one to each side of the Viper. Alisa braced herself as the strands grew in size, elongating themselves into something she most certainly recognized—snakes.

Black keeled scales glistened in the dim light as two serpents the size of pythons positioned themselves next to their master. Triangle-shaped heads with crimson eyes swayed back and forth, hissing, ready to attack.

Sarah moved closer to Travis, trying to shield herself from the snakes. With her free hand she gripped the back of his t-shirt so tightly she thought she might pull it off. It was all she could do to keep from screaming and making a run for it.

Without thinking, Sam threw the poker he had been holding at one of the snakes. With incredible speed, the snake struck at the poker, its mouth open and its fangs protruding. Its jaws closed on impact as its powerful muscles contracted and snapped the weapon in half like a brittle piece of wood.

The second snake reared its head, ready to attack. Sarah screamed out, no longer able to hold it in. She ducked behind Travis and squeezed her eyes shut. All at once a loud rumble shook the walls of the house. Hanging picture frames fell to the ground, shattering on impact. In the kitchen, cabinets swung open as dishes slid from their shelves, crashing to the floor. The sound of pipes bursting rang out as water gushed from the walls and kitchen sink in tight thin streams, spraying everything in the vicinity.

Alisa looked to Sarah knowing her daughter was responsible for the water. She herself had done the same thing as a teenager prior to training. Uncontrolled emotions and an affinity for the elements was like fire and ice. They were polar opposites and a recipe for disaster if left unchecked. Sarah had no way to temper herself in the power of the element she was unknowingly Calling. Startled, the Viper lowered itself in a defensive position, its staff positioned across its body. The two snakes quickly recoiled next to their master, poised for another strike.

This is my chance, Alisa thought. "Stay behind me!" she told the children. Quickly, she swung her hand forward as if she was reaching out for something in front of her.

"Nara!" she yelled, her voice clear and precise.

Behind the Viper, the door of the grandfather clock swung open, revealing a large staff. It flew from its slender crevice, soaring into the air, past the Viper, and toward Alisa.

The children ducked as the staff flew in their direction. Alisa caught it readily in one hand, spinning it around until it was pointed directly at the Viper.

Awestruck, Sarah fell to the ground, staring at the small sapphire sphere at the end of her mother's staff. More pipes burst in the kitchen and the walls rumbled once more.

Chapter 9

Before the Viper could react, a large eruption of blue energy burst from Alisa's staff. Streaking across the room in the blink of an eye, it struck the Viper dead center in its chest and exploded in a barrage of pale blue and blinding white light. The blast lifted the creature off its feet and sent it flailing backward into the hallway.

The Viper landed with a thud as it crashed into the staircase. Its body thrashed violently; something was spreading over its armor, moving rapidly like a parasite attacking its host. White vapors began to plume from its body. The Viper stiffened, his range of motion dwindling as blue and white ice covered his body. The ice was so cold it seemed to be burning through the bone-like armor of the Viper and into its flesh. It roared in agony before bursting into crimson flames and vanishing into thin air. Flurries of dark ash drifted to the ground where it had lain.

Travis stared at Alisa in disbelief and then turned to Sam. Their eyes met and at that very moment they knew. The box, the letter, the elemental symbols, it all made sense now. Alisa Dalcome knew magic and she could use it!

A roguish grin spread across Travis's face.

"Dude, your mom's a Jedi," he whispered to Sam.

Sam didn't reply. He could only stare wide-eyed at the weapon his mother was holding. Her staff was positioned beneath her right arm as if she were holding a large rifle. Blue and white wisps of vapor trailed from the end of sapphire stone like smoke from a gun.

The gemstone was held in place by three prongs in the shape of a lion, a goat, and a snake.

The three animals resonated with Sam, but he didn't know why, not at first. Then it came to him—his Greek mythology report from last year. It was a chimera, a fire-breathing female monster with a lion's head, a goat's body, and a serpent's tail. But a chimera could be any variety of three animals, he remembered.

It was so strange to see his mother standing there holding something so otherworldly in her hands. It reminded Sam of how much he didn't know about his mother and her past. It also reminded him that what he did know was probably a lie. Sam's chest tightened at the thought; it pained him to think she didn't trust him.

The sound of water spewing from the pipes brought Sam back to the here and now. He looked over at Travis who stood motionless, searching for anything out for the ordinary now that the Viper was gone.

"Mom ..." Sarah whispered, still sitting on the floor next to the fireplace. "How, did you do that? How did you make that thing fly?" Sarah's voice seemed calm but she was far from that, Sam noticed. Her pupils were dilated to the point where her eyes almost looked black.

Alisa didn't answer; her face was stern and focused. Her eyes moved from side to side, scanning the room, searching for any trace of the Viper.

Travis reached down and held out his hand to Sarah. "Come on, let me help you up." But Sarah didn't move. She just continued to stare at her mother.

"Sarah," Travis whispered, "take my hand. It's okay." Finally Travis's voice broke her reverie. Shaking her head, Sarah slowly placed her hand in his. She was still trembling. Travis lifted her to her feet and then looked her in the eyes.

"We are going to be okay, you hear me?" It took a second, but finally Sarah nodded. Travis smiled reassuringly.

"Mom, are you okay?" Sam asked, but Alisa still did not answer. "Mom?" Sam asked again.

"Stay behind me. Do not move from my side," she said sternly, still staring ahead.

"I think you killed it, Mom," Sarah said, holding onto Travis's arm and peering over his shoulder.

"No, it's still here, I can feel it," Alisa whispered back.

There was a bright flash from the kitchen followed by a crack. The circuit popped and all the lights went out. Immediately the sapphire gem on Alisa's staff illuminated, immersing the room in a blue tinge.

"Mom ..." Sarah gasped.

Alisa's stare intensified as if she saw something the others couldn't. "Nara," she whispered, "it's here, close by. I can feel it moving against the air. Do you feel it?"

But no one answered, at least no one Sam could hear.

"Mom," Sam whispered, "who are you talking to?"

"Shhhhh," Alisa snapped.

Sam looked over at Travis and Sarah, but all he could see were the whites of their eyes, intensified by the blue glow of his mother's staff.

Sam looked down and watched his mother reposition her grip on the staff. It was at that moment he saw the staff vibrate.

"I'm scared," Sarah said softy, reaching down and taking Travis's hand. Travis had been scanning the room closely but he stopped when he felt Sarah's hand on his. He looked back at Sarah, who stared back at him.

"Sorry," she whispered, her eyes pleading with his.

Travis squeezed her hand gently. "We're going to be okay," he said again.

Alisa had not spoken for the past few minutes; she and Nara were too busy scrutinizing the dark room, looking for the Viper. Her grip on Nara tightened as she braced herself for the inevitable.

Then out of nowhere came a hiss from the darkness just beyond the hallway. Alisa turned, Nara flashed, and a crack like a whip rang out around the room.

Sam felt a gust of wind erupt from his mother's staff, followed by a loud explosion on the other side of the room. Shards of polished wood, vertical spindles, and pieces of the handrail from the staircase blew back into the living room where they stood.

Sarah yelped and squeezed Travis so tightly his hand started to turn blue. The sounds of wood creaking and pipes bending could be heard from the second floor and water began to drip from the ceiling.

"Sarah, listen to me," Alisa finally said. Her voice was

soft but stern. "You must suppress your fear. You need to remain calm. Calm places you in control."

Those words, her mother had said something like that before. "What? Mom, I ... I don't understand," Sarah stammered.

Alisa moved Nara from side to side in a sweeping motion, trying to feel the Viper on the air. "Yes you do. You know what I'm talking about. You can feel it—you can feel the water."

Hearing this, Sam and Travis looked at one another; Travis raised one eyebrow and Sam shrugged his shoulders, baffled.

But Sarah wasn't baffled. She was scared. But she knew her mother was right. She could definitely feel something. It was as if the water was an extension of her body that she could not control. Like an arm or leg that would jerk on its own and she was powerless stop it. She could feel the water but she could not move it. It was below her in the ground. She could feel it above her too. It was everywhere. She could feel the moisture in the air moving all around them. It was like a sixth sense that had finally awakened within her.

"Sarah?" her mother said. "Concentrate."

Sarah's mind was racing now and her heartbeat began to quicken. Her anxiety was taking over. She didn't know if she could do this, not on her own. She didn't know how.

But there was no mistaking the urge from within; it was pulling at her, wanting her to connect with it. Sarah swallowed hard and tried to relax by taking deep breaths through her nose but it wasn't working. She was too scared.

"I can't do it, Mom! I can't! I'm sorry!"

"Sarah, calm down, it's okay," her mother said. Then suddenly Alisa's head snapped to the left.

"Quickly," she said, "Everyone take my hand, it's coming!" Alisa held out her hand. Sam, Sarah, and Travis looked at one another, frightened. "Quickly," Alisa said again, "take my hand!" Together they placed their hands on hers, just as a blaze of green fire burst from the darkness and sped toward them.

Instantly, everything went dark as their surroundings were swallowed up into a single flash of blue light from Alisa's staff. Sam felt like he was falling off a cliff. His stomach dropped, followed by a wave of pressure so vast he thought his bones would split from his skin. He gritted his teeth; he could barely breathe. He saw nothing but darkness, then all at once a small sliver of blue light reappeared in the distance. Suddenly Sam was racing toward it. He closed his eyes, bracing himself for impact and then ... and then nothing.

Sam opened his eyes and was astonished at what he saw. He was standing with Sarah, Travis, and his mother upstairs in Sarah's bedroom. *How in the world ...* he thought. *How did we ...* Sam looked over at his mother and sucked in a quick breath. She had done this; his mother had made them disappear into another room.

Alisa stood defiant, eyes locked in front of her, one hand on her staff and the other holding on to Travis, Sarah, and Sam. At that moment Sam forgot that his life was in danger, he forgot about the thing that was hunting them, and he forgot to be scared. He was consumed with the notion that his mother, this petite woman standing next to him whom he had known all his life could use magic, powerful magic! Travis was right, she was a Jedi!

A loud thud rang out followed by a scuffling noise on the ground that snapped Sam back to reality.

"Sam, help him up," Alisa said without looking down, as if she knew what had happened. Sam looked down to see Travis lying face down on ground.

"I'm okay, I'm okay," Travis repeated, panting and trying to get to his feet.

"Oh my God, Mom, did that just happen? Did we just ... disappear?" Sarah cried out, still holding her mother's hand.

Sam grabbed Travis by the arm and helped him to his feet. "Wow, I didn't see that coming. I must have blacked out," Travis said, bracing himself against the wall.

"Ya think?" Sam replied.

Sarah turned her attention to Travis. "Are you okay?" she asked, looking into his eyes to make sure he could see her.

"Oh, yeah, I'm fine. It happens all the time when I vanish into thin air. It's like a mild transporter accident except I rematerialized all in one piece." Travis grinned at his *Star Trek* reference. Frowning, Sarah turned, grabbed Sam by the shoulder and began with a barrage of questions.

"What is he talking about? Have you done this before? Sam, what's going on?" But before Sam could answer she turned to her mother. "Mom, how did you do that? How did you—" she looked over at Travis, fumbling for the right word, "transport us?" Sam almost smiled, but he held it back. "Someone say something!" Sarah pleaded. Travis opened his mouth to speak but Alisa interjected.

"Be quiet, all of you, and get down!" she ordered.

They all moved to the side of the bed and crouched

down next to it, catty-corner from the doorway. The blue glow from Nara was the only light in the room.

"Nara, be silent," Alisa whispered, and the blue light of the gemstone went out. Sam looked at his mother and then at Sarah. He had so many questions and he knew Sarah did too, but he didn't know where to begin. There was only one question that mattered now.

"Mom, why can't you make us disappear out of the house?"

Alisa looked over at Sam and met his gaze. His eyes moved rapidly, searching her face for answers. Alisa could see her son was confused, but he was holding it together. *Just like his father,* she thought, *always calm under pressure.* For a brief moment her heart sank. This was not the way she intended for them to find out about their past. Sam and Sarah deserved better than this.

"I can't. The Viper has placed a Binding spell on the house. No one can get in or out."

Sarah frowned and shook her head in frustration, "A what? What's a Binding spell? Mom, what does that even mean? You're not making any sense. None of this is making any sense!" she said.

Alisa looked over at Sarah, who had just about reached her limit. She needed to keep her calm before she brought the whole house down around them.

"Honey, I know it doesn't, but there isn't time. That thing out there is a hunter, and right now it's hunting us. The only way we stay alive is if we keep moving. Do you understand me?"

Sarah didn't say a word. Her face had gone white now.

"Sarah," Alisa said again. She reached out and shook her shoulder. "Do you understand?"

Sarah eyes blinked in acknowledgement, but as she opened her mouth to speak the room erupted in flashes of green fire that exploded on the wall next to them. Quickly, Alisa planted Nara firmly in front of her and the staff came to life once again in a blue blaze. Streaks of green fire shot through the darkness from beyond the doorway, heading right for them. It was too late to move, the fire was upon them in an instant. Sam closed his eyes and braced himself for impact. Sarah screamed and Travis turned, placing himself between the oncoming fire and Sarah. The sheer force of the explosion rocked the confines of the small room. Green sinuous flames curled around the huddled mass like long fiery tentacles. Sam felt the jolt beneath his feet but nothing more; he had expected to feel the hot flames engulf his body, but nothing happened. He opened his eyes and suddenly he became very still. Just inches away, shimmering in the darkness was a magnificent blue transparent shield that radiated from his mother's staff. Sam's lips parted in amazement, Sarah's body stiffened, and Travis glanced around to see if the others were seeing the same thing he was.

Alisa was down on her knees. Both her hands were gripped around her staff, which was braced against the side of her body. Before anyone could speak another barrage of fire balls exploded against the shield, which began to crack with the impact of the attack. Sam flinched and watched in amazement as the pieces of the magical shield fell away like shards of broken glass, dissolving into thin air.

"Sam!" his mother yelled. He was barely able to hear her over the explosions against the shield. "When I give the word, you and Travis take your sister and get to your room."

"What? No!" Sarah yelled, "We can't leave you!"

Sam's eyebrows drew together. "Mom, what are you saying? What about you?" he asked desperately.

"I'll hold it off. We need to buy time! If I know Xavier it won't be long before he breaks the spell!" *And Xavier is here,* she told herself. There was only one person she knew that ate Becker's Famous Chocolates, and he was not from this world.

Sarah grimaced, "Who? Who's that?"

But Alisa did not reply. Her focus was on Sam.

"Sam, ready?" she asked. Her pained stare caught Sam off guard. He didn't know what to say.

"Sam, answer me! Are you ready?"

Sam swallowed hard and nodded in agreement.

Three oncoming fire balls struck the failing shield like missiles. Alisa flinched, her muscles straining as she tried to keep her grasp on Nara, who trembled violently under the onslaught of explosions.

"No, Mom, no! PLEASE!" Sarah screamed.

Alisa gave Sam one final look. "NOW!"

Alisa spun Nara in her hand like a large baton, sending the hilt of her staff crashing down on the bedroom floor. A shockwave of billowing blue flames erupted, obliterating the bedroom wall between her and the Viper, and hurling shards of wood, wires, and sheetrock in the monster's direction.

Sam and Travis took Sarah by the hands and sprinted toward Sam's room through the hole in the wall. Flashes and sparks of electricity skewed their vision as they dove into the bedroom.

The house shook violently and the floor began to crumble and crack beneath Alisa and the Viper. She tried to brace herself but it was too late. The floor buckled and gave way, sending Alisa and the Viper tumbling into the dark abyss below.

CHAPTER 10

Sam, Travis, and Sarah slid to the back wall of Sam's room as the rest of the second story collapsed behind them. The house shook with such force that the floor beneath them rumbled and large plumes of dust billowed in through the doorway. Sam straightened himself against the wall, wincing as he moved his shoulder in a slow circular motion. A few scratches from the other night at the caves had opened up again and were bleeding now. Travis had positioned himself against the wall and was trying to help Sarah to a sitting position. It was completely dark, except for the small traces of moonlight that penetrated the tattered blinds.

"Sam, what about Mom? We have to go back!" Sarah said, trying to catch her breath.

Sam looked to the doorway and tried to steady his racing heart. From where he sat it looked as if the entire second floor had disintegrated in the blast.

"Mom," Sam gasped. The thought of losing his mother made his stomach roll and his chest tighten.

"Guys," Travis said, his voice cracking, "I ... I think we have a bigger problem at the moment."

What could be bigger than his mother trapped downstairs with that monster, Sam thought. He looked over at Travis; his eyes bulged and his mouth was gaping open. Sam's eyes met Sarah's and together they followed Travis's gaze.

In the opposite corner of the room was a huddled mass. At first Sam was not sure what it was, and then he realized it was a man. But how was that possible? Sarah had been in the house all day and he and Travis had been in the garage. There was no way he could have entered their home without someone seeing him. The man was trembling and his hands covered his head. His knees were tucked so close to his chest that it was hard to tell exactly how big he was. The outline of his body was clearly visible in the shadows, but what caught Sam's attention were his shoes—they looked familiar. They were ragged leather boots that were cracked and weathered. The left boot was missing the front part of the sole, revealing a filthy red sock. It was that boot in particular that Sam remembered.

Sam swallowed hard. Sarah reached across Travis, who sat between them, and nudged Sam's arm.

"Who ... who is that, Sam?" she whispered. Her voice was quiet with panic.

Sam stared for a moment at the crumpled man. What he wanted to say was *How should I know,* but the truth was that he did know.

"I ..." Sam hesitated. It just sounded too bizarre. It didn't seem possible. How could he get in here when nobody else could get in or out? Sam swallowed again. "I think it's Ernie."

"Who?" Sarah asked.

"Dirty Ernie?" Travis said.

"Yeah, I think so." Sam replied.

Travis let out a sigh of relief and put his hand to his forehead. "Holy crap, dude, I thought it was one of those Grim Reaper things. I was about to have a heart attack."

Sam didn't say a word. He agreed with Travis though, a Grim Reaper would be worse. He continued to stare at Dirty Ernie. Something was not right. Ernie began to whimper, repeating the same word over and over.

"No ... no ... no ..."

"Sam," Sarah whispered again. "How did Ernie get up here?"

Sam leaned forward to get a better look at Ernie. He wanted to see his face, but that was impossible because of the way the man was cradling himself in his arms.

"I don't know ..." he replied.

"I thought Mom said something about a spell and that no one could get in."

Sam lowered his head, staring at Ernie as he answered his sister. "She said no one could get in or out."

Travis slowly inched himself closer to the back wall. "I've got a bad feeling about this," he muttered.

So did Sam but he couldn't wait around to feel better about things. He needed to find his mother. He braced himself against the wall and got to his feet.

Sarah frowned. "Sam, what are you doing?"

"I'm going to talk to him," he whispered.

"Are you crazy? 'Cause I'm pretty sure Dirty Ernie is!" she hissed.

Sam didn't answer; he didn't have time to explain. All he knew was that he was running out of time. His mother was out there somewhere, possibly injured, and he had to find her.

"Where are you going?" Sarah said again. She was trying her best to keep her voice down but was failing miserably.

Sam looked down at his sister. "Shhhhh, I'll be fine. I'm just going to see if he's okay. Besides, we've got to find Mom. I'm not going to just sit here."

Travis got ready to stand too but Sam put a hand up. "No, stay with Sarah, just in case."

Travis looked up at Sam, frowned and shook his head. "Sam, Sarah is right. Dirty Ernie is crazy. He eats trash for a living, for God's sake. That says something about a person!"

"I know, I know," Sam replied. He was becoming frustrated now. "But I've got to do something. Stay with Sarah."

Travis sighed. "Then here, take this." He reached over Sarah, grabbed a piece of the charred banister that was lying on the floor next to her and gave it to Sam. "And buddy, whatever you do, don't miss," he said.

Sam smirked and took the charred piece of wood in his hand. It was heavy, about two feet long, with three broken sharp spindles attached to its end.

Sam hid the piece of wood behind his back and turned his attention to Ernie, who was still muttering "No" under his breath. Sam took one careful step forward and then another, slowly inching his way through the darkness to the other side of the room.

As Sam approached, it became clear that the man before him was definitely Dirty Ernie and that he did not look well. Dressed in a tattered black t-shirt and frayed jeans, Ernie was dressed the same as he was most days. The only thing missing was the long black coat he normally wore.

"Ernie," Sam whispered. "It's me, Sam. Sam Dalcome."

But Ernie wasn't listening; his harsh voice kept repeating "No, no, no," like he was slowly going insane. As Sam got closer, thin wiry muscles contracted in his arms, pulling his head down lower to his knees. Trembling, he began rocking back and forth.

Sam almost felt sorry for the man. Maybe he'd had an episode and lost his memory or something. But that didn't explain how he got in Sam's house, or in his room for that matter.

"Ernie, how, how did you get in here? Do you know where you are?" he asked softly so as to not frighten the man. Sam felt like he was talking to a small child who had lost his way.

Travis and Sarah craned their necks to get a better look. From where they sat they could only see Sam's back. Sarah was gripping Travis's arm again.

"I can't see a thing. What's happening?" she asked.

But Travis couldn't see much either. "I don't know, but Sam's getting closer," he whispered.

Ernie was breathing harder and rocking faster now. He seemed to be getting more agitated the closer Sam got.

"Ernie, can you hear me? Are you okay?"

Then the man abruptly stopped as if he had heard his name for the first time. Sam froze and his pulse quickened.

Slowly, Ernie began to unravel his arms from around his head. His emaciated limbs unfurled like thin spider legs emerging from a deep dark crevasse.

Sam stood rooted to the spot. His hand tightened around the piece of wood he was holding behind his back.

Ernie slowly lifted his head to face Sam. The tendons in his neck strained and a visible pulse throbbed just below his ear. A long open gash ran down the side of Ernie's jaw line. Dried blood covered his chin and the right side of his face. His gray dreary pupils twitched from side to side, as if he was searching for something or someone in the empty room.

Sam struggled to catch his breath. He felt his skin tingle as every hair on his arm stood at attention. Ernie's mouth opened, exposing gray elongated fangs that dripped with saliva.

"Nooo," he hissed.

Alisa opened her eyes to a haze of dim lights. At first she couldn't tell how many lights there were. Her right temple throbbed; a trail of pain seared its way across to the back of her head. She closed her eyes once more and then opened them again. Now there was only one dim light in the distance.

It was dark. The smell of scorched wood and dust lingered in the air, like a thick undulating fog. She coughed and felt a sharp pain on the left side of her body. Closing her eyes again, she winced and bit down on her lip. She was lying flat on her back and could feel something heavy across her legs. Slowly she lifted her head, straining to get a better look at her surroundings. Pain shot through her body, traveling from her abdomen to her lower back.

She gritted her teeth and took short shallow breaths. Quickly, she scanned the room. Silver iridescent veins of moonlight cascaded from the living room window through the billowing clouds of dust. Water continued to gush from the ruptured kitchen pipes, creating a fine mist that lingered in the stale air.

Debris from the blast littered the living room. Mounds of wood and sheetrock lay in heaps around her. Wires and scraps of insulation clung loosely to severed floor joists above her.

Gasping, Alisa eased her head back to the ground. The agonizing pain was almost unbearable. She waited a few seconds before gradually taking another breath.

But this time the air smelled different. There was something more than dust and wreckage there. It was the smell of iron; it was the smell of blood. Alisa knew that if she could smell the blood, chances were that she had lost a lot of it.

Slowly she turned her head, tilting it just enough to see her midsection, but it was too dark to see anything clearly. The large support beam and part of the staircase that lay across her legs obstructed the moonlight.

Alisa leaned her head back down and listened intently. She could not hear anything over the spewing water in the kitchen. She didn't know if that was a good thing or a bad thing. Did the children make it? Were they safe? She had to find out.

She needed Nara, but where was she? Alisa looked around the room to the best of her capabilities but Nara was nowhere in sight.

"Nara," she called out, her voice strained and raspy. She brought her hand to her mouth and coughed. When she pulled it away, she grimaced. A thick dark liquid oozed down the length of her palm.

Blood, well, that's disappointing, she told herself.

"Nara," she cried again, this time a bit louder.

In the distance, just beyond the debris, a familiar blue glow appeared in the darkness. "Nara," she gasped as a weary smile fell across her face. *There is still a chance.*

Carefully, Alisa slid her hand down the side of her body to the injury. She could tell she had broken a few ribs, but even worse was the thin shard of wood lodged between two of them. If she had to guess, it was between rib six and seven. She could feel the sharp shaft protruding out of her body but she was too weak to grab it.

Alisa pursed her lips and closed her eyes. She took several shallow breaths and braced herself for the pain.

"Nara!" she yelled. With the cry her body cringed and her lungs constricted. She clenched her jaw and felt her muscles contract around the wooden shaft. The pain was excruciating.

Out of the darkness a blue light sped toward her. Alisa tried to lift her hand to catch the staff but she couldn't; she no longer had the strength. Nara bounded over the wreckage but she fell short and landed on the ground next to her.

Alisa turned, her breathing labored. She could see Nara's sapphire hilt just inches away from her hand. Her familiar dim glow was soothing but Alisa was too weak to move, she had lost too much blood. With her arm outstretched, she called once more a barely audible, "Nara ..."

The staff responded as it always had and snapped into her open hand. Instantly the symbiotic connection took effect, and Nara knew what her master needed. Alisa felt the rush of Nara's healing race through her body. Her heart quickened and her muscles began to tingle as blood coursed through her veins. Alisa knew in the end it wouldn't be enough to heal the wound completely, but it was enough to stop the bleeding and restore her vitals to a normal level.

Within minutes, Alisa could move again. She twisted in pain as she pulled the spike out of her side. She closed her eyes, breathing quickly as she waited for the wound to close. Within minutes, Nara had healed her. She was still in pain but was on the mend now.

Alisa positioned her hand underneath the large wooden beam that lay across her legs. Just as she began to lift, two flashes of light illuminated the back of the living room. Still trapped, Alisa froze.

"Nara, silent," she whispered, and Nara obeyed.

She listened closely; she thought she heard voices coming from the back of the living room but she wasn't sure. It was still hard to hear anything over the gushing water. But then she heard them again—voices, she was sure of it. Was it Xavier? If it was, who was with him? It wasn't the Viper; they didn't speak that she knew of.

There was only one thing Alisa knew for sure: she had been compromised. Her role as a sleeper agent had come to an end and there was no telling who was after her now.

The intruders began walking around the room, their feet crunching on the scattered wreckage that was once her home. They were coming closer. Alisa could feel a rush of adrenaline but she wasn't sure if it was her or from Nara, who was vibrating intensely in her hand, awaiting her command.

Alisa gripped Nara so tight her knuckles had turned white. They were almost here; they were almost on top of her.

CHAPTER 11

Sam took another step back. His legs felt weak and his hands were trembling. Quickly, he brought forth the piece of wooden banister he had been holding and grasped it firmly in his hands. Behind him he could hear Travis warning him.

"Not Ernie, Sam, not Ernie!"

"Sam, get away!" Sarah yelled as she got to her feet.

Sam blinked rapidly. His hands were clammy and shaking as he repositioned his grip on the wooden shard.

"Travis, keep Sarah back!" he said.

But Travis had already gotten to his feet and was standing in front of Sarah, protecting her from whatever was in the room with them.

Ernie slowly rose, and as he did, his body began to change. Long, slender arms morphed into thick, twisting muscle. His gray, pallid skin hardened, changing from flesh to a flat black exoskeleton marred with thin black scales.

Sam stood mesmerized, lost in the creature's transformation. Believing in magic was one thing; watching it destroy someone he knew was almost unbearable. He wasn't prepared for this. He had never known anyone in his life that had died until today. Watching Ernie being ravaged from the inside out made his stomach turn.

Sam thought he could hear voices somewhere in the distance telling him to move away. But he couldn't run; there was nowhere to go, nowhere to hide. He couldn't leave Sarah and Travis there. Not alone, not with this ... this thing.

A low, resonating growl brought Sam back to reality. The creature's unrelenting gaze was bearing down on him now. His jaw hung open, revealing a row of savage-looking teeth. A long strand of saliva dripped from his mouth onto the floor. His head began to jerk and his teeth snapped. He looked deranged, like a rabid dog.

The hard exoskeleton was slowly spreading across his face now like a virus, infecting every human cell he had. The skin around his eyes began to expand and tear away, revealing swollen, reptilian orbs the color of blood.

Sam steadied himself and took in a deep breath, gripping the piece of wood as hard as he could. *This is it,* he told himself. *You have no other choice. Sorry, Ernie, if you're in there.* Sam reared back and swung the piece of wood as hard as he could.

The wood came around like a baseball bat, moving so fast that it was no longer visible. A loud smack reverberated around the room, and the monster stumbled as its head careened into the side of the wall. The tip of the banister shattered upon impact, leaving Sam with a fraction of the weapon he once had.

Shaking, Sam took another step back as the monster turned to face him once more. Its lower jaw had become unhinged by the blow and it dangled at an odd angle, making the beast look even more menacing than before. Sam shuffled backward, his wide eyes watching the beast. Its jaw bone cracked and popped as it realigned itself beyond its human confinements. Frayed and contorted skeletal tissue began to regenerate, fusing torn gums to splintered teeth. Sam wanted to turn away; he could feel the excessive saliva building in his mouth followed by the taste of something sour, but he kept facing forward.

Sarah shuddered in fear as she watched Ernie's grotesque transformation unfold in front of her. Quickly she scrambled across the wood floor to the corner of the room. Travis followed closely behind. The house groaned and from his bathroom Sam could hear the slow twist of pipes expanding and contracting.

He moved cautiously around the bed but he was running out of room. Sam bumped into the dresser and slid along the back wall and window.

The monster glared at Sam, then slowly turned to look at Travis and Sarah. They both stood nestled in the corner. Tears were streaming down Sarah's face and Travis held her tight.

Sam moved away from the window toward the back corner of the room but he stopped when he saw something glimmering on the floor behind the monster. His eyes narrowed and then he realized what it was. It was the small shovel Travis had taken from the fireplace set. He must have dropped it when they ran into the room.

"Travis, by the door!" Sam hissed.

Travis's eyes were fixed on the monster but he looked back to the doorway when he heard Sam's voice.

The monster heard his voice and turned its attention back to Sam. Sam stared at the creature his mother had fought earlier. It didn't make sense. *How did that thing escape the blast? Unless ... unless it didn't.* Sam could feel his blood turn to ice. *Unless there are two!*

Sam stared more intently at the creature that stood before him. Its long flowing cloak had reappeared, fanning out over the hard wood floor. Sam could hear the horrid hiss that accompanied it and he looked for the snakes but didn't see any. Until he looked at the creature's arm.

There, coiled around its forearm, was a long, black, slender snake. Sam swallowed hard. From the corner of his eye, he saw Travis inching his way behind the monster, heading for the shovel. Sarah remained frozen, huddled in the tight corner of the bedroom.

Sam needed to keep the Viper's attention on himself. He needed to buy Travis some time. They would only get one shot at this; their very lives depended on it.

The Viper's large gloved hand took the thick snake and pulled it from its wrist. The long serpentine body twisted and spun within its grasp. The Viper slowly turned its head and focused its attention on the snake, which immediately stopped moving and lay still in its palm. It was as if they were communicating. Sam watched as the snake stiffened. Fragments of gnarled bone began to surface on the snake's overlapping scales, transforming into the staff Sam had seen earlier.

In the shadows, just beyond the Viper, Travis crept across the floor on his hands and knees until he reached the shovel. Reaching out, he grasped it in his hand. He looked up, first at the Viper, then at Sam, who was pinned in the corner with nowhere to go.

Travis wiped the sweat from his brow and carefully got to his feet. In the corner, Sarah covered her mouth with both hands to keep from screaming. Her eyes bulged as she glanced between Sam, Travis, and the Viper.

The Viper inched its way closer to Sam, turning its staff sideways as it walked. One hand was on the center of the shaft, the other on the snake-like pommel. Slowly, the Viper pulled the staff apart, revealing a long, slender, single-edged sword.

Sam's eyes grew larger, his mouth fell open, and his body went rigid. The majestic sword had a distinctive curve that reminded Sam of a Japanese katana sword. He recognized the style from his Ninja Warrior 5 game. The blade was an eerie black that somehow seemed to shimmer.

Sam's gaze darted between the Viper and Travis, who was slowly approaching the creature from behind. Sam hoped Travis's distraction would work; that it would give them time to get past the Viper and make a run for it. To where, he wasn't sure, but any place was better than here.

"Sarah, get ready to run!" Sam called out.

Sarah nervously dropped her hands from her face and, still clinging to the wall, inched her way toward the door. Sam's eyes moved from his sister back to the menacing creature that towered before him. The Viper stopped just a few feet away from him and raised its menacing sword. The sinuous muscles contracted beneath its skin-like armor and Sam heard the Viper's gloved grip tighten around the hilt of the sword. He braced himself, preparing for the inevitable.

Travis inched closer, planting his left foot firmly on the ground. Then he twisted his body and pulled the shovel back over his shoulder. Sam could see his forearms flex as he repositioned his hands around the slender handle. Seconds felt like minutes, until finally Travis took in a deep breath and swung the shovel at the monster's neck.

A loud metallic *pang* rang out, jarring the creature, but it recovered quickly and spun around and clipped Travis's legs from underneath him with the sheath of its sword. Travis flew into the air and landed with a thud on his back.

Sarah stopped running mid-stride. "Travis!" she yelled.

Sam saw his opportunity and took it. He ran shoulder first into the Viper. It was like hitting the side of a house. The collision pushed the Viper's arm into Sam's left side, causing the sheath to fall from its hand. Sam felt an agonizing pain streak across his shoulders and down his back. Losing all forward momentum, he staggered back, dumfounded, and almost lost his balance. Sam tried to reach down to help Travis, who lay sprawled out on the floor, but it was too late. The Viper had regained its footing, spun around, and grabbed Sam by the neck.

"SAM!" Sarah screamed.

The Viper held Sam over its head. Gasping, Sam instinctively grabbed the Viper's wrist and began to jerk and twist, trying desperately to wrench himself free. But it was no use; the creature's grip was like a vice, choking the life out of him.

Travis winced and rolled onto his side, clutching his back. Sarah moved closer but Travis held up a hand.

"Sarah, stay back!"

He got to his knees and stood, bracing himself against the wall. But just as he turned, the Viper backhanded him with the pommel of its sword. Travis flew back against the wall again and slid onto the floor. He clutched his throbbing nose, which was bleeding now. Sarah ran to his side and together they turned to Sam.

Sam gasped for air as his feet dangled helplessly above the ground. His face was red and his lips were blue. He could feel the Viper's grip gradually tightening, constricting the blood flow to his brain. His vision blurred and his eyes bulged like they might burst from their sockets. The Viper snarled like a savage beast, its wicked red eyes wild with hatred. Sam heard Sarah's terrified scream as the Viper moved the tip of its blade to the front of his chest.

CHAPTER 12

Alisa lay as still as possible, taking slow, controlled breaths to calm her heart rate. She stared wide-eyed up at the scorched ceiling, praying that no one would find her. She could still hear the footsteps as they approached, each step bringing the intruders closer and closer. Alisa tightened her grip around Nara as she held her against her chest. Looking around, she noticed a change in the room. The moonlight that had streamed through the window a moment before had vanished and was replaced by a tall, dark, foreboding shadow. Alisa's breath caught in her throat and her body stiffened.

"Where are they?" a voice whispered. It sounded female but Alisa could not tell for sure.

The intruders were moving just beyond the pile of debris in front of her. Her body was barely visible from where the strangers stood but her legs were still buried beneath the shattered staircase, making it impossible for her to move. Her head was the only thing not covered by some sort of wreckage, but it was still hidden in the shadows of the room.

"I don't know. But it doesn't look good," the man said. He was whispering too but that didn't hide his thick Irish accent.

That voice, Alisa thought, *that accent.* Her heart quickened. *Was it, could it be, Xavier? Did he break the Binding spell?*

"The staircase is completely destroyed. We'll need to search upstairs for survivors," he said.

Alisa could feel the butterflies in her stomach. It was Xavier! She was sure of it now.

She lifted her head to get a better look when Xavier quickly raised Ian and a bright emerald light burst from the darkness.

"Who's there?" he called out.

Alisa held up her hand to shield her eyes.

For a moment no one spoke. The only sound was that of the gushing water spilling from the broken pipes in the kitchen. Finally the woman asked, "Lees, is that you?"

Her voice was soft; she had an accent but it was hard for Alisa to tell if it was familiar or not through her whisper.

Alisa nodded eagerly. "Yes," she gasped. "Yes, it's me!"

"Ian, be silent," Xavier said, and the bright light went out.

"Nara," Alisa said, and a soft luminous glow radiated from her staff, revealing two familiar faces. For the first time in thirteen years Alisa stared back into the eyes of friends, people from her home world.

"Alisa!" the girl cried, her voice full of anticipation.

"Holly? Holly Quinn?" Alisa was brimming with excitement. But she didn't have to ask; she would always recognize those almond-shaped eyes staring back at her. A warm feeling radiated through her body and she could no longer contain her grin.

"Yes! It's me, it's me!" Holly said as she dug through the debris to get to Alisa. Xavier joined in lifting the large support beam she was stuck under, and rolled it to one side.

Alisa finally stood and Holly flung her arms around her so fast that the two of them almost fell over again. They both giggled and laughed like school girls. Alisa had forgotten about her wounded side until Holly mentioned it.

"Oh, Lees, you're bleeding!" she said.

Alisa looked at her abdomen. The blood had soaked the right side of her uniform but it looked worse than it felt now that Holly was there. She smiled back at Holly. "I'm fine. I'm better than fine now."

Xavier stood idly by, watching as the two childhood friends reconnected. It had been so long since they had seen one another, and for thirteen years they had both lived with the knowledge that they had lost each other forever.

Alisa was wild-eyed and glowing; she had not felt this happy in years. Holly, who was fighting back tears, hugged Alisa again, squeezing her tightly. Alisa winced, but she held on tightly.

"Oh, I missed you, Lees!"

Holly stepped back and Alisa stared at her dear friend, drinking in every feature. Holly looked exactly the same as she had thirteen years ago. Her eyes were still majestic, glimmering blue, purple, and pink against her flawless porcelain skin. Her pronounced cupid bow lips were spread wide in a giddy grin. Thin wavy strands of coal black hair dangled beneath her hood down the sides of her high cheek bones, like they had when she was younger. Alisa sighed heavily, placed a hand to Holly's soft cheek, and smiled. She fought back the twinge of sadness that surfaced within her. They had missed out on so much, she thought. Their lives had turned out to be nothing like they'd planned.

It wasn't until Xavier cleared his throat that the two women finally stopped gushing over one another.

Alisa turned, still smiling, to see the gruff old Keeper frowning like he always had. Xavier had changed over the years; he had been a strong, brawny man the last time she had seen him, but now he looked thin and a little worse for wear. His rugged, vibrant features were gone, replaced by deep-set eyes and frown lines that made him look twice his age. Short white whiskers covered his broad jaw line now, but his gray ill-kempt hair was as unruly as ever. Some things never changed.

"Xavier," Alisa exclaimed. Her gaze had turned serious as she stared into his hazel eyes. "I knew you were out there. I knew you wouldn't give up."

A roguish grin etched its way across Xavier's rough exterior and the center of his hollow cheeks turned pink. Holly snorted, "My my, Mr. Ward, either your lip has gotten caught on your teeth or that's a smile I see."

Xavier's eyes cut to Holly and his grin faded into a thin line.

"What?" Holly asked. She smiled, shrugging her shoulders.

Xavier turned his attention back to Alisa. "And just how did you know it was me, dearie?"

Still smiling, Alisa said, "Why, the chocolate wrappers of course."

"You see?" Holly interjected. "I told you, you have a serious sweet tooth. It's a problem, Xavier; you should see someone about that."

Xavier rolled his eyes. "There is no problem. We don't even know if they were mine or not," he said, looking back at Holly.

"Okay, okay, there's no problem. They are clearly not yours," she conceded, shaking her head.

Satisfied, Xavier turned his attention back to Alisa.

"And how did you find my—" his eyes cut to Holly, "—the wrappers, might I ask?"

"I didn't, Sam did ..." Suddenly the reality of everything that had happened came rushing back to Alisa and the color drained from her face.

"The children!" she gasped. She turned to Holly, panic stricken. "Sam, Sarah, Travis—have you seem them?"

Holly shook her head just as a distant scream rang out over the gushing water.

"SAM!"

They all turned to look upstairs.

"Sarah," Alisa gasped. Sarah was calling Sam's name and she sounded terrified.

Nara immediately began to glow, followed by the two other staffs. But it wasn't because of the danger upstairs—it was because of the danger behind them.

The room ignited in a fiery green blaze as three balls of fire sped toward Xavier, Holly, and Alisa. The first two exploded into the wreckage next to them, sending shards of debris in every direction. The remaining fireball headed straight for Alisa. Acting on impulse, Xavier shoved Alisa aside as the fireball exploded in a blinding emerald blaze.

Alisa and Xavier fell on top of the debris as Holly turned to shield them with her staff. A continuing barrage of fire soared across the room, exploding against Holly's violet translucent shield. Between the bright flashes of light and the thrashing impact of the fireballs against her shield, Holly searched the room for the Viper. But it was too dark; there was no sign of the creature and the fireballs seemed to materialize out of nowhere.

Alisa rolled to one side behind a large section of the staircase. "Quickly, Xavier, over here!" she yelled.

She watched as Holly braced herself against the onslaught of explosions, her shield slowly disintegrating in front of her. Alisa looked back over the rubble to Xavier, but he had not moved. He was lying face down in the debris.

A fireball exploded to the left of Alisa and she ducked as wood and sheetrock rained down on her. "Xavier!" she called out again, huddling against the staircase for protection. "Quickly!" But there was still no response. Holly's shield was close to failing now; only a glowing sliver of light remained, and then suddenly everything went dark.

The sound of rushing water and heavy breathing were the only noises in the room. Holly quickly moved back, taking shelter behind a large piece of flooring that was perched on a small pile of wreckage.

Crouched down with her back against the pile, she took in a deep breath. "Noah, be silent," she whispered, and the violet light when out.

Alisa could feel the back of her neck tingle as she poked her head above the rubble and scanned the room for the

Viper. It was dark again, except for a thin ray of moonlight that shimmered off the water-drenched floor. There was no sign of the Viper. It seemed to have vanished.

Slowly, Alisa began climbing over the debris, inching her way closer to Xavier.

"Xavier," she called out. Her voice was filled with a mixture of fear and dread, but there was no answer.

Alisa moved to Xavier's side, placed two hands on his shoulder, and gently turned him over. Xavier's limp body fell across her lap and her eyes met his empty gaze.

"No," she gasped. "No ..."

Quickly, she began looking for Xavier's staff. *I need to find Ian,* she thought. *Ian will save him.* Her eyes searched the debris around them but she didn't see the staff. She began to panic and moved Nara closer to the wreckage.

"Nara, light!" she commanded.

Nara's soft glow grew brighter and that's when she saw it. Just a foot away from Xavier's outstretched hand, Ian, like his master, lay dark and unresponsive.

A lump formed in Alisa's throat. She shook her head in disbelief, running a shaking hand down the side of Xavier's cheek. His skin was already cool to the touch and his complexion was rapidly fading to a waxy gray. She promptly began to look for a wound. Maybe it wasn't as bad as she thought, she told herself. Maybe he was just unconscious and Ian could heal him.

But Alisa stopped, frozen by the sight of a large burnt gash that had been carved out of Xavier's midsection. Her eyes filled with tears and her lip began to quiver. She had seen this type of injury several times before in the Great

War. The wound had been cauterized by the blast, so there was no blood—just a glittering green residue around its outer edges. The residue was venom from the Viper's fire ball. Each blast was a deadly mixture of fire and venom. Alisa could tell by the color of Xavier's skin that the venom had moved into his heart and was now spreading into the outer regions of his body.

This cannot be happening. This isn't real, she told herself. *This is Xavier Ward.*

Alisa looked over at Holly, who had tears streaming down her face.

"Is he ...?" Holly choked.

The despair in Alisa's face answered her question, but she nodded anyway, wiping the tears from her eyes. "Yes."

Holly's eyes went dull as she lowered her head.

Another scream rang out from above them and they both jumped, startled by the noise.

Alisa looked up to the second level.

"My children!"

She turned back to Holly, who was staring at her now. "Go, I've got it down here," Holly said.

Alisa nodded, got to her feet, and, with Nara blazing in one hand, she evaporated from the room.

Sam struggled against the grip of the Viper. The pressure inside his head was mounting; his vision faded as the outer edges of the room began to ebb away into a deep foreboding darkness. The sword was almost at his chest. The creature had positioned the tip of the glimmering black blade directly over his heart.

"Noooo!" Sarah screamed, looking on in horror. She was holding onto Travis who was bleeding from his nose.

A fine mist filled the air from the burst pipes in the bathroom. The water vapor moved like an emerging cloud wafting through the room. Sam's grip was failing, slipping little by little, until his hand fell from the Viper's arm. He had no strength left, only hope. Hope that he would pass out before the beast stabbed him with the sword.

As Sam's eyes began to close, a flash of blue light burst into the room.

Alisa emerged through sapphire wisps of smoke. Her hand was outstretched, pointing toward the Viper. The other held Nara close to her body.

White swirls of mist began to spin around the Viper's arm that held the sword. The Viper paused and looked at Alisa, confused. Its arm began to shake; its muscles tensed as the whirlwind of water spun faster and faster. Sam could feel the monster's grip loosen as the sheer force of the whirlwind pushed it to the ground. The Viper struggled and its sword hand shook as it tried to move the blade closer to Sam's chest.

Travis and Sarah stared up at Alisa in astonishment. She stood with her hand guiding long swirling ringlets of white mist from her hand to the Viper's arm.

Suddenly, the Viper's grip gave way and Sam fell to the ground, gasping for air. The Viper's entire body was now engulfed in the swirling tentacles that dragged it to the ground. Sam slowly began to crawl across the floor until he reached Travis and Sarah.

Alisa closed her hand into a tight fist, releasing the last of the swirling tentacles into the Viper. Like a caged beast, the monster tore, craned, and pulled at the mystical whirl-winds that confined its body, but to no avail. Alisa looked down at the children; they were safe, at least for now. Sarah's eyes were red and swollen, Sam's face was slowly regaining its color, and Travis, who was still holding his nose, had blood covering his hands, neck, and throat.

Her heart twisted inside her chest to see her children and their friend in such pain. This was her home, her children, and she was supposed to protect them. But she felt powerless. The Great War had followed her here; this monster had tracked her down and was trying to not only kill her, but kill her children too.

When would this ever end? She had lost so much already—her husband, her friends, her home, and the only life she had ever known. And now it wanted to take her children. *Over my dead body,* she thought.

Alisa took a step behind the children. Their frightened stares followed her every movement. She grasped her staff with one hand on each end and brought Nara down around them, encompassing them in a tight circle. She pulled Nara close until the staff rested across the children's chests. Then she moved her hands closer, pulling them into a tight embrace.

The Viper was down on its hands and knees now. It pulled and heaved against the swirling, mystical bindings, trying frantically to free itself. Only the outline of its body and its red glowing eyes were visible through the swirling mist.

"Hold on," Alisa whispered. Nara began to vibrate, and together Nara and Alisa released the element of Air that bound the Viper. The whirling mists around the beast began to fade just as Alisa and the children evaporated in a flash of blue mist.

Sam saw the twisting of light and felt the intense force of gravity pressing against his body again until he rematerialized downstairs. Alisa removed her arms from the children and took a step back. Most of the light in the room came from Nara's glow, which was dim at best.

They were all sitting on the ground except for Travis, who had toppled over to one side. He had passed out again. Sarah began tending to Travis and shook him gently until he was awake. Sam, who still felt like he had cobwebs in his head, cleared his throat. He put a hand to his tender neck, which still hurt from the Viper's grasp. He tried to swallow and almost choked. Slowly, he closed his eyes and lifted his head, turning it side to side. The muscles in his neck were sore and his body was stiff all over.

It wasn't until Sam opened his eyes again that he saw the hooded stranger standing before them and he almost choked again. The woman was dressed in a purple traveling cloak and holding a staff. Sarah and Travis looked up, startled by the cloaked figure. She was bent over a body that lay face down on the floor. Sam's eyes moved to the staff on the ground and swallowed hard. It was the same twisted staff he had seen the man carrying in front of his house. Sam looked to his mother, who oddly enough didn't seem to be scared. In fact, she didn't seem bothered at all about the two strangers in the room. His eyes narrowed as he stared at the cloaked figure.

Seeing this, Alisa took a knee next to Sam and placed her hand on his back. His muscles were tense, still reeling from the Viper attack.

"It's okay, Sam, she's a friend," she said.

Sarah quickly turned and stared at her mother in disbelief. *This ... this woman is her friend? How? Where did she know her from, and why, for the love of God, is she dressed like that?* A million questions ran through her head and nothing made sense anymore. She had almost been eaten by a swarm of spiders in her own house and her brother had almost been choked to death by Dirty Ernie, who turned out to be some kind of monster, so at this point anything was possible. Her mother could even vanish into thin air for crying out loud, so when it came to what was possible and what was not, she didn't have a clue anymore. Sarah bit her lip and decided that now was not the time for questions. Instead, she turned her attention back to Travis, who still looked squeamish.

Sam had questions of his own as he looked at his mother. But just as he opened his mouth to speak, two flashes of light emerged from the living room. He squinted and turned away, shielding his eyes until the light had vanished. From the darkness, two more strangers appeared. Both were dressed similarly to his mother's friend. Each had the same type of cloak and dark gray armor. Beneath the armor they wore some kind of dark clothing, but Sam couldn't make out anything more than that. The new hooded strangers stepped forward as wisps of colored vapors emanated from their cloaks, one blue and the other green.

They each carried a staff in one hand. The taller of the two raised his hand toward the kitchen and Sam felt a gust of ice cold air roll across his face. The water spewing from the kitchen instantly hardened into thin strands of ice that resembled long, interweaving tree branches frozen in an ice storm. The mist circulating in the air turned to snow and gently floated to the ground. Suddenly the room was quiet. All eyes were on the two newcomers who were now walking toward them.

Chapter 13

"Wow, am I seeing things?" Travis asked in a groggy voice. His nose had stopped bleeding, but he still looked a little peaked from evaporating to the bottom floor. Sarah was busy dabbing at his chin with a towel she had found in the debris next to her.

"Hold still," she whispered. Travis frowned and lifted up his chin.

The tall stranger pointed to the second floor of the house, which was more like a balcony now, and the man next to him evaporated, leaving a wake of blue mist.

The remaining stranger continued forward, stopping when he reached the group. They all stared in silence. He stood just a few feet away from them and said nothing, his head moving from side to side as he looked at each one of them. With one hand he brought his staff in front of him. It had a long, narrow black shaft with silver ornate symbols etched on its body. The pommel was a three-pronged set of wings that fanned out and tapered into sharp points at the ends. In the center of the wings sat an oval, jade gemstone.

Sam watched as the stranger turned toward the body lying

on the ground. The man sighed and reached up to pull back the hood of his traveling cloak.

"Hollister, light," the man commanded.

The jade gemstone illuminated, casting a green glow around his face. He was an older man with short white hair and a thin beard. His eyes were a dark yellow, like the color of honey, with flakes of dark green speckled throughout his irises.

The man stood there for a moment staring at the body. His hard gaze made Sam uneasy. At first he couldn't tell if the man was angry or sad until he noticed the stranger's jaw clench, and his fingers tighten around his staff. Finally, the man's gaze moved from the body on the ground to Alisa. Alisa, who looked like she had seen a ghost, stared back at the man, her eyes full of tears.

"Demetrius, you're here?" she choked out. She stepped forward, wrapping her arms around the man's neck. Sam and Sarah turned to one another, confused.

Demetrius returned her gesture with a warm embrace, closing his eyes as he hugged her. "He's dead, Demetrius," Alisa confessed. "He died saving me. Xavier is gone because of me."

Demetrius held on to Alisa. The small frown lines around his eyes seemed to fade away as he quietly exhaled. When he opened his eyes again he looked to Holly with a warm smile. Holly pulled back her hood, and for the first time Sam could see her face.

Whoever she was, she was beautiful. Her majestic eyes were filled with tears, but her expression conveyed something more. The corners of her mouth lifted just a bit when she looked back at the man holding his mother. She seemed relieved. Travis and Sarah took turns looking around the room at the strangers.

"Look at me, Lees," Demetrius said. Alisa stepped back, looking up at Demetrius's face. "Xavier left this world exactly the way he was meant to leave it—as a Keeper. Never forget that. As long as you remember him here," Demetrius placed his hand over her heart, "he will live on forever."

Alisa closed her eyes as tears streamed down her face. She nodded in compliance and forced a smile.

"Demetrius, where ... where is Gordon?" Holly asked. Her eyes searched the room, as if she expected him to surface at any moment. But the room was empty; there was no sign of Gordon. Holly met Demetrius's steely gaze and she knew. Gordon was dead.

Sam noticed the exchange between Demetrius and the woman as the room fell silent. The sadness between them made Sam feel uncomfortable and out of place, as if he was intruding on something very personal. By the look on Sarah and Travis's faces he could tell he wasn't alone. Sam looked away and fidgeted with his hands, then rubbed them down the front of his shorts.

The silence was becoming unbearable when a flash of blue light appeared several feet behind Demetrius. Sam, Sarah, and Travis recoiled in surprise as Vallen appeared from the second floor.

"Top floor is empty. No sign of the Viper," he reported to Demetrius.

Alisa looked at Demetrius. "There are two Vipers, Demetrius. They could be anywhere."

Demetrius nodded in agreement; his look was firm and confident.

"We must leave before they return. Lees, where are the remaining gate keys?"

Alisa blinked in surprise. She wasn't sure she had heard him right.

"Leave? But, where will we go?" She knew she sounded confused, and she was; it sounded so final when he said leave. Especially if he was asking for the gate keys.

Demetrius placed a hand on Alisa's shoulder. His stern expression faded, replaced by a kinder, more gentle appearance.

"Home, Lees. It's time to come home."

Alisa's lips parted at the very mention of the word and a slow smile stretched across her flushed face. Her blue eyes began to shine as she lifted a trembling hand to her mouth and whispered, "Home."

Holly smiled and took in a deep, satisfying breath. Sam, Sarah, and Travis exchanged confused glances.

Sam hated feeling like this, as if someone had shared a joke and he was the only one who hadn't gotten it.

Demetrius returned Alisa's smile and gently squeezed her shoulder. "Lees, we need the keys," he said.

Alisa dropped her hand from her mouth. "They are in my Quarrem, in the garage."

Demetrius looks puzzled. "In the ..."

Alisa gestured outside. "I'm sorry. In the small building next to the house. The Quarrem is hidden in the north wall, near the floor."

Sam and Travis shot each other a knowing look.

Demetrius looked to Vallen and Holly.

"Holly, you stay with me. Vallen, retrieve the Quarrem and check the perimeter of the house once more," he said. Vallen nodded and immediately evaporated.

"Come, Lees, you can gather your belongings later, once the location is secure."

"Mom?" Sarah said. Her voice was softer and calmer than Sam had expected. "What's he talking about? Leave? Leave where? Where are we going?"

Alisa turned to see all three children staring back at her. Their curiosity was etched in their frown lines and furrowed brows. There was so much to say, she thought. So much for them to know, but now was not the time. *Soon,* she told herself, *soon.* Right now they needed to get as far away from Earth as they possibly could. Haven was their only hope now and the Majesty was their only chance of survival.

"Sam, Sarah," she began, "there will be time for questions later. But right now you need to listen to me. We need—"

Before she could continue all three staffs began to glow at once. Holly's face went white. "Demetrius, behind you!" she shouted.

Two gloved hands appeared out of the darkness, reached forward, and grabbed Demetrius by the throat, pulling him back into a smoky void. Sam flinched as two red eyes glowed before vanishing into the darkness. Alisa spun around with Nara in hand, ready to defend herself. But there was nothing there except for darkness and few whips of lingering black smoke.

"Demetrius!" Holly screamed just as a massive green and black snake fell from the darkness above. Quickly, it slithered down the length of Holly's body, curling around her in tight coils, and hoisted her into the air and out of sight.

Alisa moved back behind the children, taking her staff in both hands again. "We're leaving. I have to get you out of here!" she said as swirls of ominous black smoke spun and twisted from the shadows, speeding toward them.

"Mom, behind you!" Sarah shouted.

Before Alisa could turn around the smoke had seized her by the wrists, dragging her high into the air above the children.

"Mom!" Sam yelled. He looked back just in time to see the Viper standing a few feet away, its arm outstretched holding its staff. Sam recognized this Viper—it was missing a glove.

"Run!" Alisa yelled as black strands of smoke twisted and slid down her arms, resting around her neck like a noose. "Run!"

Suddenly, Alisa's body flew across the room. The children watched in horror as she slammed into the living room wall. The impact jarred Nara from her grasp and the staff fell to the floor.

The Viper advanced, its red eyes bearing down on Alisa. It reached out with its free hand and Nara began to levitate off the ground.

No, Sam thought. Nara was his mother's only defense. Without her staff she had no chance. With a flick of the wrist the Viper sent Nara flying into the wreckage near the back of the room.

Without thinking, Sam sprang to his feet and jumped over the piles of debris to retrieve Nara. Travis looked over at Sarah. "Wait here, don't move, I need to help Sam," he said.

Sarah didn't respond. Her face was blank and ashen. "Sarah!" Travis yelled. He wanted her to acknowledge him before he left her side. But she just stood there in a catatonic state, staring at the Viper. He looked over to Sam, who was frantically searching for Nara, and then back to Sarah. Travis quickly grabbed Sarah by the shoulders and shook her.

"Sarah. Sarah, come on!" Sarah's gaze moved from the Viper to Travis. She nodded. With a sigh of relief Travis turned to join Sam. The wisps of smoke pulled Alisa's hands above her head, pinning them back against the wall. The black smoke around her neck began to contract, closing off her airway. She choked against the force of the smoke, gasping for any air she could get.

The Viper moved closer and withdrew its sword. Alisa's heart raced and the skin on her wrists, arms, and neck were starting to burn from the mystical smoke.

In the distance, just beyond Sarah, flashes of green and purple erupted from the ceiling and Holly reappeared, falling to the ground with a loud crash. She scrambled to her feet, throwing off the large dead snake that was wrapped around her body.

"Alisa!" she gasped.

She spun her staff forward and raised it high. Noah flashed, sending purple sparks into the air. There was a loud roar of thunder as a bolt of purple lightning burst from the staff. The Viper quickly turned and countered Holly's attack. Its black sword slashed through the air, deflecting the blast back in Holly's direction causing her translucent shield to appear. A loud explosion rocked the house and a blinding light filled the room, turning everything momentarily white.

Holly and Sarah covered their eyes as a wave of heat and gale force wind blew them off their feet and back into the wreckage behind them. The Viper turned its attention back to Alisa, who was still fighting to break free from the smoke. Writhing and pulling against her bonds proved to be useless. She grimaced in pain as the smoke bindings continued to burn her flesh. The Viper was just a few feet from her now, its red savage glare moved from her eyes to her chest as it lifted its sword.

Sam, holding Nara firmly in his fist, was the first to surface from the wreckage. Travis stood up just seconds later, but Sam was already running toward his mother. Travis rolled out from the wreckage behind Sam and made it to his feet.

Without turning, the Viper stopped them mid-stride. Black smoke appeared around their necks and Sam and Travis collapsed onto the ground, gasping for air. Nara fell from Sam's hand onto the floor, her sapphire gemstone flashing rapidly.

The Viper turned to move in front of Alisa again and brought the sword to her chest once more. She cringed at the heat of the wicked blade against her body. Her eyes moved to Nara; she tried to call her name but she could no longer speak.

Her gaze then fell to her son and his friend, choking before her, and there was nothing she could do. Determined not to give up, Alisa clenched her fist and pulled against the shackles of smoke with all her strength. But it was no use; the coils became tighter and more restrictive. Her neck stiffened and her arms trembled under the strain as every muscle went rigid in protest. She could feel her insides twisting with hatred like she had never felt before. She wanted to kill this beast, rip it limb from limb. She wanted it to feel pain, the same pain it was inflicting on the children.

She continued to struggle until she saw Sarah emerge in the distance, holding Nara in her hand. Suddenly, all of Alisa's frustration and anger turned to fear and desperation.

Sarah, no! What are you doing? Alisa knew if Sarah got too close, the Viper would sense her and turn on her. She needed to run—she needed to get Sam and Travis and run! *Please Sarah stop!*

The blood had drained from Sarah's face, leaving dark shadows around her eyes and cheek bones. She stepped over Sam and Travis, who were still grasping at the smoke around their necks. Sam held out a hand as she passed, trying to stop her, and Travis shook his head.

"No, Sarah," he choked out. "NO!"

But Sarah continued to move closer. She didn't seem to acknowledge them; her stare was fixed solely on the Viper. She trembled as she walked, moving as if she was in a trance. Sarah gripped Nara in both hands and raised the staff over her shoulder.

Alisa shook her head violently, urging her daughter to stop and run away. But it was too late; Sarah was directly behind the Viper now. She lifted Nara over her head, but before she could strike the Viper spun around and slashed Sarah across her midsection. Blood immediately began to seep through her shirt, spreading quickly into a straight line across her stomach. Sarah stumbled back, Nara fell from her hands, and for a second she stood, stunned. Her terrified eyes met her mother's before she fell to the ground.

Unable to scream, Alisa jerked and gasped at the smoke in rage. Her body twisted, thrashing violently as her daughter lay motionless on the ground.

The Viper spun with the sword in its hand and turned back to Alisa. She was panting, barely able to breathe now. Everything inside of her screamed as the tip of the blade touched her chest again. Sam and Travis watched in agony as the Viper plunged its sword forward and Alisa's body went limp.

Chapter 14

There was a flash of light followed by a loud crash as Demetrius and the Viper tumbled through the darkness. They rolled over one another until they came to an abrupt stop in front of Sam and Travis. Demetrius was the first to stand, and when he did Sam saw that he was bleeding from his neck and face. There was a long gash scorched diagonally across his chest armor. The Viper lay face down with arms outstretched, reaching for its black sword just inches away. Demetrius took a step back, twirled Hollister in his hand and brought the pommel down toward the Viper. But before Demetrius had a chance to strike, the Viper and its sword vanished. There was a loud crack and sparks of jade and sapphire burst from the pommel as it struck the empty floor.

Sam, still gasping for breath, watched as Demetrius swung his staff back around, caught it with his other hand, and lowered himself to a crouch, poised for another attack. He took long, labored breaths as he gazed erratically around the room, scouring the darkness for any sign of the Viper. He inched forward cautiously, moving closer to Sam and Travis, who were still writhing on the ground against the smoke. Demetrius was only a few feet away when it happened. Hollister flashed just before the black blade ripped through the darkness, revealing the Viper's position. The sword came crashing down from above but Demetrius raised Hollister over his head just in time to block the blade. Demetrius's legs buckled from the force of the impact, sending him down to one knee. Emerald sparks spewed from the blade's edge as it ground against the staff, sliding down between Demetrius's hands. As the blade broke free and the Viper reared back for another blow, Demetrius evaporated, leaving the Viper stupefied in a green swirling haze.

The room was beginning to spin and Sam could feel his lungs burning from the lack of oxygen. The more he struggled, the more the tendrils of smoke suffocated him. Gasping, he reached for the inky black smoke around his neck and felt nothing. His hands scraped and clawed at his tender throat but it was no use.

Helpless to do anything, Sam looked over to Travis, who was also struggling against the smoke. He watched as Travis's hands fell from around his neck to the floor. Again, Sam craned his neck back in pain and his eyes bulged. Twisted images flashed through his head—his mother being stabbed, his sister being cut down by the Viper. He opened his mouth to scream in agony but nothing came out. Darkness closed in and he could feel himself slipping away. It was at that moment, as his heart raced and his lungs starved for air, that the room erupted in a barrage of colored lights. Streaks of blue, green, and purple soared across the room. There were loud explosions, people yelling, and sparks flying as the whole room rumbled beneath him. Suddenly Sam felt the smoke around his neck give way and a rush of air filled his lungs. He gasped as the air stung his dry throat, making him choke and cough. Rolling over on to his side, he saw Travis with his hands over his mouth doing the same. They were alive.

Sam hesitantly propped himself onto his elbows, unsure if it was safe to even move now. His throat felt raw and his skin still burned, but none of that mattered when he saw Demetrius, Vallen, and Holly across the room. Holly was standing over one of the Vipers. She held Noah firmly in her hand with its pommel aimed at the remains of the beast. The creature looked frozen—its body was covered in thick layers of frost that had cracked into several large chucks.

Demetrius and Vallen stood over the second Viper and it too was frozen solid. Vallen's sapphire gemstone was pointed at its chest, emitting swirls of blue and white vapor. The frost-covered Viper sparkled in the sapphire light, its unresponsive serpent eyes glowed a dull crimson.

Sam watched as Demetrius moved from Vallen's side and began to slowly circle the Viper, his fierce gaze never leaving the savage beast. With each step Demetrius took, the gemstone in his staff became brighter and brighter until the entire room was illuminated in a brilliant emerald glow.

Demetrius moved in front of the Viper, his glare piercing and calculating. He stopped just inches away from the Viper's head and Vallen, who was standing next to him, grinned malevolently. Sam wondered if he was feeling triumphant or if he actually enjoying himself. Vallen lifted the tip of his staff from the Viper's chest and took a step back.

Demetrius took his staff in both hands and twirled it around so that its pointed wings and emerald gem were directly above the Viper's head.

Vallen and Holly both brought their staffs in front of them, preparing themselves for what Demetrius was about to do.

Demetrius raised his staff. His eyes glowed a searing yellow.

"This ends now!" he thundered.

Demetrius stabbed the frozen Viper. There was a loud boom. Sam braced himself as the walls of the house shuddered and the ground shook again. Like a brittle statue that had fallen over, the Viper's body cracked and broke apart into several large pieces. Wisps of green smoke billowed out of the corpse, sending several screaming specters in the shape of snakes, spiders, and other ghoulish things Sam didn't recognize into the air before they vanished.

Sam stared at Demetrius, who stood glowering over the remains of the Viper. The muscles in his jaw were clenched and his nostrils flared, taking in deep, controlled breaths.

Sam noticed the wounds on Demetrius's face had already healed themselves. In fact, after looking around the room, Sam noticed that none of the strangers seemed to a have a mark on them anymore. No one said anything for a few moments. Sam, who was grateful the Vipers were finally dead, could contain himself no longer. He leapt to his feet and ran to his mother's side as Travis ran to Sarah. But Sam's heart sank when he reached her crumpled body. Her skin had turned a sallow, translucent green that revealed the faintest trace of her skeletal frame. Her features had become gaunt and there were dark circles around her eyes.

"Mom ... Mom speak to me ..." Sam cried. He cupped her head in his hands. "Please, Mom, I ... I don't know what to do ..."

He reached for his mother's arm, which felt cold and lifeless. He raged with fear and frustration that tore at his insides, trying to claw their way out. He shook with adrenaline as he tried desperately to keep it together.

"Mom ... answer me, Mom!" he pleaded, his voice breaking as he spoke.

Sam gripped his mother with both hands and pulled her close, gently rocking her back and forth. Hot tears streamed down his face as he looked to Travis, who was cradling Sarah in his arms.

"Sarah ..." Sam whispered.

Travis held Sarah tightly with one arm under her back and the other over her waist. "Sarah, wake up, don't do this!" he yelled. But there was no response. Sarah's arms dangled at her sides and she didn't seem to be breathing.

The two boys, overcome with pain, looked up as the sound of rustling footsteps approached from just beyond the doorway. Demetrius, Vallen, and Holly stepped forward in unison, each brandishing their staffs in front of them. All three gemstones came to life, illuminating the room entirely. Startled, Sam and Travis looked up at one another, their large eyes bright with tears.

No one said a word as the room filled with the sounds of shallow breathing. They all watched as the knob of the battered front door slowly began to turn.

Sam and Travis were frozen in anticipation, their eyes glued to the door as it slowly creaked open.

A dark silhouette with long hair inched its way forward, past the threshold into Sam's house. Sam let out a sigh of relief as the light met the intruder's eyes. He knew this person. He recognized the green, catlike eyes gleaming in the staff light. Standing in his doorway, with an elusive look on her face, was the girl from next door. Sam's eyes quickly flashed to Demetrius, Vallen, and Holly who had crept behind the door, ready to strike.

"Wait!" he said abruptly, holding up his hand. "I know her." The girl looked startled as her eyes moved to Demetrius and the others pointing their staffs in her direction. Then her gaze fell on Travis and Sam, who were clinging on to Sarah and Alisa.

The girl timidly stepped forward, her eyes cutting back and forth between Alisa and Sarah.

"We mean no harm; we are here to help you, Samuel," she said, looking directly at Sam. The sensuous tone of her voice was soothing and made Sam feel less hesitant about her being there.

Sam stared at the girl as he drew his mother closer in his arms. How did she know his name?

"We are friends of your parents. Please, let us help you. Time is of the essence."

"*We?* Who is we?" Demetrius grunted as he lifted his staff a bit higher.

The green-eyed girl eased the door back to reveal a tall, gangly man standing just beyond the threshold. He was well-groomed, dressed in black slacks and a white collar shirt. He wore a tie that hung loosely around his neck, and it looked like he had just returned from work. He surveyed the room curiously before pursing his lips into a forced smile.

"This is Jacob," the girl said. The man nodded nervously and his pale skin turned a rosy red. Sam thought that maybe he was her father, but who calls their father by his first name?

The girl turned her attention back to Sam, who wiped the tears from his face.

"Samuel," she persisted, "please, we can help." The sincerity in her voice helped ease the apprehension that was building up inside Sam. He looked to Demetrius for reassurance. After all, he was the one with the weapon trained on her. But to his surprise Demetrius had already lowered his staff.

Sam turned back to the girl. He could hardly see her through the tears that filled his eyes. His voice cracked when he tried to speak. "It ... it killed my family. They're ... all gone."

The girl inched into the room. "Please, Samuel, let us try to help."

She took one step forward, then another, inching her way toward Sam and Travis. Neither of the boys moved; they both sat on the floor, quietly watching as she approached them. Holly and Vallen lowered their staffs as the girl grew closer.

She knelt down next to Sam and placed a warm hand on his shoulder. "Samuel, I promise I won't hurt them," she said. "We need to lay her on the ground, okay?"

Sam's swollen eyes met hers. He wasn't sure if it was her jade green eyes or her angelic features that calmed him, but without realizing it he had relinquished his mother into the girl's arms.

She placed a hand underneath Alisa's body and laid her gently on the ground. Sam winced, looking at the small cauterized wound in the center of his mother's chest. The same green glimmering poison that had been in Xavier's wound traced the edges of the gash.

Everyone stood quietly watching as the girl removed a small vial of amber liquid from her pocket. She quickly flipped the top off with her thumb and placed the tip to Alisa's pale, parted lips. The thick liquid poured freely into Alisa's mouth until the vial was empty.

"We need to help your sister as well," the girl said. She looked at Sam, as if asking for permission. Sam wiped more tears from his eyes and gave a gentle nod. The girl turned to Jacob, who seemed hesitant to enter the room and remained rooted to his spot by the door. "See to Samuel's sister," she said firmly.

Jacob nodded and moved quickly across the room to Travis. "Please, I need to help her," he said. But Travis was reluctant. He held on to Sarah's hand, staring into the man's somber face. Sam knew Travis was in as much pain as he was; he cared for Sarah and he was scared. But Sam also knew if there was any chance of saving his family, any chance at all, they would need this man's help. "Travis ... it's okay, let them help," he said.

Travis looked at Sam. His cheeks were tearstained and his hands still trembled, but he slowly released his grip on Sarah so Jacob could take her.

Sam turned back to the unusual girl as she stared at his

mother's pallid face, hoping for any sign of consciousness. He watched as she took her hand and gently stroked a few loose strands of his mother's hair back against her head. A few days ago Sam thought this girl was just an ordinary teenager like himself. *Boy, did I get that wrong,* he thought to himself. He stared at the girl as she tended to his mother. Long, straight strands of raven black hair fell across her heart-shaped face, accentuating her apricot skin. Her long eyelashes batted like small wings around her eyes, which vigilantly moved between Alisa and Sarah.

She looked kind of exotic, Sam thought. He had never seen anyone quite like her before. But that wasn't all—she looked too confident in what she was doing, as if she had done this before, and that gave Sam cause for concern. For one, she knew his mother, and two, she knew Sam by name. He wondered what kind of magic she possessed. She wasn't carrying a staff, so maybe her magic didn't work that way.

There were so many questions but none of them really mattered right now. All that mattered was that this girl, whoever she was, could potentially help his mother and sister. Sam's stomach was in knots and he couldn't keep his hands from shaking. He wanted to help, but didn't know how. He wasn't even sure what they were doing.

"What's happening? What are we waiting for?" Sam asked impatiently between sniffles.

The girl did not move. She continued to stare down at his mother's body.

"Sometimes our eyes can deceive us and things are not as they seem, especially when black magic is involved," she said in an even tone. "This tonic," she held up the vial, "better known by my people as Soulrista Immortalalice, will tell us if her spirit is alive. If the spirit lives, then there is hope."

"What do you mean *your* people?" Travis asked.

Everyone's eyes moved to Travis, except for the girl's. She continued to stare at Alisa. Sam looked up to Demetrius, Vallen, and Holly, who stood behind Travis. Holly's face was streaked with tears and she looked down and began shuffling her feet. Vallen stared at Travis nonplussed, as if he wasn't expecting a question like that just yet. Demetrius, on the other hand, narrowed his gaze. Sam wasn't sure what he was thinking. He was much harder to read than the others.

The room fell silent until Vallen finally said, "There will be a chance for questions, but now is not the best time."

Scowling, Travis returned his gaze to the floor where Sarah and Alisa lay. Sam felt his frustration too; his questions seemed to be mounting by the moment and no one was answering them. He looked down at his mother and sister.

"No," Sam said a little louder that he intended. "I think now is the perfect time." Travis looked up. "I think someone needs to tell us who you people are and why you are here!"

Sam's face had gone red, as anger swelled inside of him, twisting into a giant acrimonious knot that lodged in the center of his chest. If he didn't say something now he thought he might explode.

"Now is not the—"

"No, now *is* the time! I don't even know this girl's name," Sam said, glaring at Vallen. Then his eyes moved to the green-eyed girl.

"No," the girl interjected. "Samuel is right; he needs to

know." She took a deep breath, tucked her hair behind her ear, and looked up at Sam. Her ear was thin, long, and unusually pointed.

"My name is Lyra and we are not from this world," she said bluntly.

Sam mouth fell open and Travis's eyes grew twice their regular size.

"I'm—"

"Vulcan!" Travis blurted out and slapped his hand over his mouth. He looked just as shocked as Sam felt.

Lyra frowned, confused. Sam's eyes cut to Travis.

"What?" Travis groaned "She said 'not from this world.'"

Lyra slowly tuned to Sam and continued. "I am Elvin, and we," she swept her hand toward Demetrius, Holly, and Vallen, "are from a world called Haven."

Sam stared at Lyra for a moment, not saying a word. He couldn't believe it—first magic and now this. What was next, dragons? Sam felt his whole body go numb. He had seen his mother do magic and that would mean his mother was from another world too. Sam felt his head begin to throb. He placed his hand on his forehead and ran it down the length of his face. *Secrets,* he thought, *so many secrets.*

Sam didn't say anything for a moment. He wasn't sure how to respond. He wasn't sure about anything anymore. His life had been turned upside-down in a matter of days, each day more awful than the last.

Finally, in an effort to change the subject, Sam asked, "How will you know?"

"Know?" Lyra asked, bewildered.

"How will you know if she's alive?" he asked, staring at

his mother with a blank gaze. His voice was monotone and distant.

Before she was able to answer, Jacob turned and looked up, "Lyra!"

Sam turned to Jacob. Specks of golden dust sparkled in a ghostly golden glow around Sarah's body like a fine mist.

"That's how," Lyra said. "That is her soul, you see. It's faint, but she is alive." Jacob reached down and lifted Sarah's bloodstained t-shirt off her stomach. The thin gash across her midsection had vanished, leaving only a dark scar in its place.

There were tears in Travis's eyes, but he was smiling and Sam couldn't help but smile too. His sister was alive! She had made it, which meant there was still hope for his mother too. He saw Demetrius step forward out of the corner of his eye. Sam looked up at him, but his smile quickly faded. Demetrius wasn't looking at Sarah; he was gazing down at Alisa.

Sam turned to see Lyra lower his mother's head back to the ground. Her despondent gaze made Sam's heart seize up, and the sick, empty feeling crept its way back into his chest.

"What," Sam asked, "What is it? What's—" But his voice caught in his throat when he looked down at his mother's body again. Her skin seemed paler than before, and there was no golden glow or sparkling anything around her body. Petrified, Sam looked to Lyra, but her once luminous green eyes were vacant and sad now.

"I'm sorry, Samuel, I am so ... sorry." He could hear the finality in her voice.

Sam shook his head. "No, no, please, you've got to do something, please!"

He moved closer to his mother and took her hand. "Mom!" he yelled. "Mom, please, you can't leave us, you have to wake up." Tears began to steam down his face again. "Mom ... Mom!"

Sam looked up at Demetrius with a wild panic in his eyes. "Do something! You have to help us!" he yelled.

Holly gasped and covered her mouth, her eyes welling with tears. Travis held Sarah's hand and stared at Sam's mother. His eyes were swollen and red.

Sam slowly placed his head on his mother's chest and through broken sobs and trembling shoulders continued to mutter, "Please, please ..."

CHAPTER 15

It was some time before Sam left his mother's side. Holly finally persuaded him to move to the couch, giving Lyra and Jacob space to attend to the bodies, which they covered with large blankets. Sam watched from the corner of his eye; the sight of his mother and Xavier just lying there made him feel empty and absolutely miserable inside. Travis looked just as bad as Sam felt and he would not budge from Sarah's side. His swollen nose and two black eyes from the fight with the Viper made him look like a sullen-faced raccoon. Despondent and exhausted, Travis stared blankly into Sarah's pale face, oblivious to his surroundings.

The living room was still fairly dark, except for the light from the two staffs, which illuminated various parts of the room. Demetrius, who felt the need to secure the perimeter as soon as possible, had instructed Vallen to return to the cave and report back to the Majesty. Vallen was to request reinforcements, Healers, and someone from Magical Sterilization to come back to the house.

The power was still out and it was beginning to get warm inside. Stale air hung like a thick blanket over the room and the ice sculptures Demetrius had created earlier out of the spewing water from the pipes were beginning to melt. Sam's and Travis's faces were glistening with sweat.

Holly sat with Sam in silence on the couch, the pair of them lost in their thoughts. Sam crossed his arms as his mind flickered through flashbacks of the awful battle that had claimed his mother's life. It was still hard for him to wrap his mind around the fact that she was really gone. He kept replaying the moments before it happened, before the Viper took her life. *How could this be?* But more importantly, why them? What had they done to deserve this? There were eight people, four of whom could use magic, fighting against two Vipers and they still could not stop the beasts from killing. *What good is magic if it can't save the ones you love,* Sam brooded.

He stared at the remains of the Vipers in disgust. No one had touched the beasts since their demise. Sam had overheard Demetrius talking about waiting for someone or something to show up and dispose of the bodies. It made him sick to look at these creatures in his house. He was glad they were dead; he was glad he got to see them die, but there was a part of him that wished he had been the one to kill them.

Sam could finally feel something now—he could feel hatred writhing inside him, swelling to a point where it was almost impossible for him to sit still. It wasn't enough to see the vile creatures slain to pieces, he wanted more. He could feel his face flush with anger. His body felt like it was on fire, like it could burst into flames at any moment. He looked around the room but everyone was occupied.

Demetrius was alone in the kitchen standing guard. Lyra and Jacob were huddled together by the front window. Travis was still by Sarah's side and Holly sat next to Sam in a daze. Then there was the Viper that Demetrius had stabbed, its destroyed head lying just inches from its body, which glistened with frost. A single crimson eye lay on the ground next to the Viper's head, still frozen, staring back at Sam. He tried to look away but he could feel its cold, penetrating gaze taunting him. *I'm still alive*, it seemed to say.

As Sam looked past the Viper, he noticed its sword off to the side. The eerie, black blade was absent of all color and light. Sam stared at the outline of the weapon, but there was no visible matter that could be seen—it looked as if part of the floor was missing, replaced by a thin black void. Sam felt the power emanating from the slender, single-edged blade, as if it were calling to him. His mouth felt dry and he winced as he swallowed; his throat was still sore from the Viper's black magic.

He gritted his teeth just thinking about what it had done to his family. It had killed his mother, critically injured his sister, and now it was mocking him, staring at him as if he was next. Sam could feel sweat begin to pool on his forehead and the back of his neck. His hand twitched in small spasms as the urge to act intensified. He wanted the sword—he wanted to feel its power in his hand. He could feel it beckoning him, longing to be a part of him.

Before Sam knew what he was doing, he had leaped from the couch and darted across the room before anyone could stop him. He reached the Viper's body in seconds and the sword flew into his open hand. Holly sprang to her feet but froze in her tracks, stunned at the crazed look in Sam's eye. Demetrius lunged forward, a look of horror etched across his face.

"Sam, NO!" he yelled.

But it was too late. Sam wasn't listening; he was lost, consumed by his own rage, his desire for vengeance too great. He slashed wildly at the Viper's broken body with the ominous black sword. His eyes blazed with fury and malice. He could feel the rush of adrenaline, like molten fire burning its way through his body. The sensation was exhilarating—he had succumbed to his hatred and it felt good.

"You killed my family!" he shouted. "You. Killed. My. Family!" Each devastating blow to the Viper was more powerful than the one before. Travis stared in shock before turning to shield Sarah and himself from the flying bits of frozen corpse that flew their way.

"You. Killed. Her! You. Killed. My. Mother!"

Holly stepped forward but Demetrius waved her off. "No, Holly, don't!" he said, too captivated by what he was witnessing to even look her in the face.

Holly forced herself to stop just a few feet away from Sam. Her delicate features were twisted with fear and frustration.

Lyra had moved cautiously toward Demetrius, her eyes trained on Sam.

"Demetrius, the sword," she whispered. On the surface Lyra's voice seemed calm, but Demetrius noted the edge of unease in her tone. "It should have ... killed him."

Demetrius said nothing. He stood mesmerized, but Lyra

was right. To grasp a Viper's sword was fatal. Blistering burns would appear on one's hand, as if it had been plunged into blazing fire, followed by infection and a swift death. But Sam seemed to be unaffected.

Sam continued to swing the sword like he was possessed, not stopping until every piece of the Viper's body had been eradicated. Completely exhausted and out of breath, he fell to his knees with the sword still clutched in his hand. He took in heaving gulps of air as he stared down at the Viper's sword. The blood had drained from his face, leaving him looking washed-out and fatigued. His eyes were stuck in a vacuous stare that was fixed on his quivering hands.

"It took my family," he said between ragged breaths.

He looked up at Holly. "It took my family!" he shouted, tears welling in his bloodshot eyes.

"Sam, please," Holly said, reaching out to him in a desperate plea to console him.

"No, I don't understand!" he shouted, shaking his head angrily and dropping the sword. "What did we do? We did nothing wrong!" His desperate plea for understanding was more than Holly could take. Her unrelenting anguish had reached the surface and she found herself clutching her chest.

"Sam, please!" she implored, "Let me help you. I can—"

"You can what?" Sam yelled, rounding on her. "Are you going to tell me more lies? Because that's what she did!" He pointed to his mother lying on the ground, covered by a blanket.

"Sam, please," Holly begged, her voice breaking as reached out for him again.

"My whole life has been a lie, hasn't it?" he cried, glaring at Holly. Holly was silent, scared of saying the wrong thing. "Hasn't it?" he asked, turning his frantic frustration on Demetrius. Demetrius remained calm, his face suffused with sympathy, but still he said nothing. Sam stared scathingly into the Keeper's eyes. "Answer me!" he demanded. "Answer! Me!"

"It was for your own protection," Demetrius said finally, taking a step closer to Sam. "She wanted a better life for you, a normal life for you and your sister."

"Protection?" Sam shouted back with a look of disgust. "Protection!" He laughed belligerently and wiped the tears from his eyes. "Did you hear that, Travis—protection!"

Travis looked sad and abashed. "Sam, don't ..." he pleaded softly.

But Sam looked back at Demetrius. "Well, she failed and I lost everything! But you didn't lose a thing did you? Did you?" he asked, pointing his finger before turning to Holly, "None of you did!" He waved his hand hysterically. "Your lies destroyed my family and they are never coming back. Never!"

Rocking back on his knees, Sam lowered his face into his hands. Holly quickly rushed to his side and brought Sam into a tight embrace. Sam burst into uncontrollable sobs as his body shuddered with the outpour of emotion.

"I never got to say I'm sorry ..." he said between sods. "I never got to say it."

Holly leaned her head against his, "Oh, Sam," she whispered, fighting back her own tears.

"It hurts," he muttered softly, finally embracing Holly. "It hurts so bad."

As Sam's vulnerability swept through the room, Lyra slowly turned away toward the window, her eyes glistening. Jacob followed her, looking more uncomfortable than ever, and Demetrius stepped back into the kitchen, his poignant gaze remaining fixed on Sam and Holly.

Travis was speechless. He and Sam had been on the same page for such a long time, both having parents that died. Over the years they had endured the emptiness together. They had felt the loss, but they were each too young to remember the heartache and sorrow that accompanied the death of a loved one. Over time, that loss had forged a bond and they had grown to count on one another. But now things had changed; Sam had lost someone whom he had known his whole life. Someone he loved and it pained Travis to think that Sarah might be next. That she might suffer the same fate as her mother. He stared down at Sarah and resigned himself to silence. He knew what Sam needed most was time—a few hours alone to sort things out, and that's what he was going to give him.

CHAPTER 16

In the hours that followed, the unnatural quiet began to take its toll. What little hope they clung to regarding Sarah ebbed away in the bitter silence. Her pale-skinned, comatose state was a constant reminder of the devastation they had suffered at the hands of the Vipers. Within a single evening Sam's life had been ripped apart—his mother killed, and his sister critically injured. Now he sat in a room filled with dead bodies and strangers whom his mother had called friends.

Time felt like it was moving backward. Sam was tired of just sitting there; he felt like he should be doing something to help his sister. The living room had become deathly quiet, too quiet, even for Sam. But that all changed in an instant.

From the back of the room three bright flashes appeared, followed by four more in a haze of blue mist. Sam almost jumped out of his seat as Vallen emerged with a rucksack, removing the hood of his traveling cloak and holding his staff out in front of him.

Sam could not help but notice the cavalier smirk across his face. For the first time, Sam was able to see the man behind the cloak. He had long, brown hair and gray eyes that cautiously surveyed the room. Vallen seemed different, Sam thought. He wasn't like the rest of his mother's so-called friends. He was confident but there was a silent arrogance about him too. Where Holly and Demetrius seemed caring and sympathetic, Vallen looked distant and calculating. There was also a noticeable difference in the staff that he carried. Vallen's staff was not straight like the others. Instead, it had three sharp curves in its shaft. Where the others had sphere-shaped gemstones as pommels, his was a diamond held in place by two talons. Sam watched as Vallen moved across the room with a quick, determined stride. He was definitely the most aggressive of the three and Sam felt it was best to keep his distance when possible.

There were six tall strangers who accompanied Vallen, all cloaked and holding staffs. But these men did not look like Demetrius, Vallen, or Holly either. Their cloaks were cobalt blue and they were dressed in elegant silver armor with a crest of a star in the center of their chest. Their helmets, which concealed their faces, had large wings on either side. Each soldier held a long, silver staff with a sapphire and silver pommel the same shape as the unique crest on the chest plate.

Vallen continued to walk purposely toward Demetrius as the men behind him spread out throughout the bottom floor of the house. Sam quietly observed the scene before him. He felt drained and his muscles were weak from swinging the Viper's sword. If it weren't for the fact that his sister was lying unconscious on the floor and his home was being invaded by armored soldiers from another world, he felt like he could sleep for days.

Travis frowned and narrowed his eyes as he moved closer to Sarah. He didn't seem at all comfortable with the new batch of strangers. His brutish glare went unnoticed by Vallen and the two approaching soldiers, who split off to cover both exits. Sam and Travis both eyed the three soldiers in the back of the room as they quickly evaporated again, reappearing upstairs with a flash, one in each room. The last soldier stood silently in the center of the living room. Sam couldn't help but stare at him as he gazed around the room with a confident stare. He looked like a superhero or a gladiator, but without the sword.

Travis sat with his feet crossed on the floor holding Sarah's hand, locked in a catatonic stare. His mouth had fallen open and his head began to sway as he scrutinized the soldier. Sam, who had seen enough magic to last him a lifetime, was not so taken aback by the armed guard standing in his living room, but was more concerned with what they were doing there. Looking for answers, he inched his way closer to the only stranger he felt comfortable with—Holly.

"Who are they?" he whispered, sounding calmer than he actually felt.

But Holly seemed more distant now than she had been before. Staring at his mother's covered body, she tuned to face Sam. He could tell she was trying to hide her emotions as she forced a smile. But he saw past her brave front into her mournful eyes. The pain there was real. Hidden just beyond the swirls of pink and blue lay the agony she felt, the raw knowledge of knowing her friend was never coming back.

"Centurions," she said softly as she turned back to stare at his mother. Sam opened his mouth to ask what exactly a Centurion was, but he thought better of it. She was clearly in no mood to talk about soldiers and quite frankly, neither was he.

Vallen approached Demetrius, who was standing in the kitchen with one hand on his staff and the other tracing the finer edges of Alisa's Quarrem. He stopped and stood for a moment, observing Demetrius. He was in deep thought and seemed unaware of Vallen's presence. Vallen grimaced; he had not expected this upon his return, considering he had just arrived with the reinforcements Demetrius himself had requested. Demetrius scowled. His lips were pursed and his eyes seemed intent on burning a hole in the Quarrem he was staring at. Before asking the obvious, Vallen looked to Lyra and Jacob talking in hushed tones across the room and frowned. His eyes then wandered to Holly and the boys huddled around the couch. Vallen rubbed the base of his neck and sighed in exasperation before turning back to Demetrius.

"Um, everything all right?" he asked, perplexed by the scene in front of him.

Demetrius lifted his gaze to look a Vallen. "What?" he asked, a bit dazed.

Vallen's gray eyes narrowed as he motioned to the rest of the people in the room. "Did I miss something? What happened?"

Demetrius's troubled gaze moved from Vallen to Sam. "It's the boy," he said flatly.

Vallen turned to Sam and Holly, not exactly sure what he

was supposed to be looking for. They both looked grief-stricken. "Oh, well, yeah," Vallen murmured, "it can't be easy on him."

"No," Demetrius said sharply, "that's not it."

Vallen turned back to Demetrius. "It's not?"

Demetrius's stare intensified and his vibrant amber eyes filled with concern. "The boy held the sword."

Vallen's face went slack. Surely he had not heard Demetrius correctly. "What? The sword, you mean ... the Death Sword?"

Demetrius nodded slowly.

Vallen looked awestruck and he turned to look at Sam again. "But that's ... impossible, I mean, he seems unharmed. He's not ..."

"Dead?" Demetrius supplied. "No, he's not dead."

"But ... what does that mean?"

"I'm not sure, but there is something extraordinary about this young man," Demetrius said earnestly.

"Like his father, perhaps."

Vallen and Demetrius turned to see Lyra approaching them. "He too was extraordinary, and his mother was as well. They were both Chimeras, I believe," she said, knowingly.

"And just how did you know that, exactly?" Vallen asked with a scowl.

Catching his tone, Lyra raised an eyebrow bemusedly and stopped in front of Vallen. Jacob was close behind her.

"Well, Chimeras are quite rare aren't they? Only a handful exist, isn't that right, Demetrius?" she said with a mischievous grin. Her eyes moved in a pretentious stare, first to Demetrius and then the pommel of his staff.

Vallen smirked, "Oh, is that right?"

Lyra returned his smirk with a glare. "Yes," she said coldly.

Jacob stood behind Lyra, quietly fiddling with his tie. The palpable tension in the room was making him nervous. Lyra and Vallen stared at one another for several more seconds before Jacob finally spoke up.

"Well," he choked, "maybe we should talk about the children." He looked to Lyra and Vallen, hoping his meager attempt to defuse the tense situation would go unnoticed.

"Who is this, Lyra?" Demetrius asked, his skepticism etched in the deep lines running across his forehead.

"Oh, I'm sorry. Jacob Montgomery," the man said with timid smile as he held out his hand.

"Yes, but what are you doing here, human?" Vallen hissed.

Jacob's grin quickly faded and his hand fell to his side. "Well I'm—"

"That's classified," Lyra interrupted, her hard stare still fixed on Vallen. Vallen's lip curled in agitation.

"Well, I'm afraid we'll need to know more than that, Lyra," Demetrius said cooly, his tone a bit sharper this time.

Lyra's green eyes moved slowly from Vallen to Demetrius and she forced a smile. "Well, if you must know, he is the human liaison for the Elvin Empire."

Demetrius's eyes grew wide and Vallen's mouth fell open. "What?" he gasped, clearly outraged. "The Elves are working off-world?"

Lyra casually turned her attention back to Vallen, not trying to hide the sardonic grin that was spreading across her face now. "That's classified."

"There is one working portal, Lyra and no one knew about it until a few days ago," Demetrius said, "not even the Elves. So how exactly did you get here?"

"Also classified," she said again, not taking her eyes off Vallen. Vallen was fuming now; his face was flushed and the blue gemstone on his staff had begun glow.

"Well," Jacob said nervously, his eyes shifting back and forth between Lyra and the two Keepers. "Perhaps we should talk about the staffs again."

Vallen's eyes cut across to Jacob and he took in a deep breath. "It's classified," he said smugly.

Vallen turned to Demetrius. "The Healers and Coppertop will be here soon enough and then we can get out of here," he said as he handed his rucksack to Demetrius. "For the Quarrem."

Demetrius took the rucksack and placed it on the counter next to him. "I'll be with the Centurions if you need me," Vallen said. His steely gaze had moved back to Lyra now. "I need some fresh air." He pulled the hood of his traveling cloak over his head and left.

They watched as he evaporated and reappeared on the top floor. Jacob stared up at him in admiration. "Amazing," he said. His eyes were lit up like a small child's at Christmas.

"Yes, well, I don't think he likes me much," Lyra said with a lingering smile, still looking up at Vallen.

"No, it's not that," Demetrius said dismissively. "He hates all Elves equally."

Lyra's eyes rolled to Demetrius, "Thanks, I feel much better now."

Demetrius smiled mischievously. "It's good to see you, Lyra."

"It's good to see you as well, old friend," she replied with a warm smile.

"So, what can you tell me? Why exactly is the Elvin princess so far from home?"

"Well," she said, "I can't tell you much. I wasn't lying when I said it was classified. But let's just say that the Majesty is not the only ones with sleeper agents."

Demetrius's jovial expression disappeared and his brows pulled together into a more concerned look. "Do you mean the Elves have been here the entire time?"

"No, not the entire time," Lyra said. "But long enough to establish an alliance with the humans, and long enough to find out about Alisa and the children."

"I don't understand. Why Earth? Why come back here?"

Lyra's emerald eyes looked crestfallen and Demetrius noticed the hesitation in her voice when she spoke. "There is a war brewing, Demetrius. It's at our door step—all the signs are there, just like before. But this time it will be far worse. We will not be fighting a common enemy—we will be fighting ourselves."

Demetrius's expression became dark as his well-defined face pulled into a tight scowl. He knew what she was talking about. Bellisoria had been warning them about this for some time.

"The Majesty is weak at best, and now," Lyra whispered, looking over at Sam and Holly, "well, let's just say that this is what they have been waiting for. The catalyst for war; the justification needed to implement plans that have been in the works for several years."

"You still didn't answer the question, Lyra. Why Earth?" Demetrius asked again.

"Perhaps we should refrain from saying anything more," Jacob cautioned, giving Demetrius a sympathetic look. "I'm sorry, Demetrius, but this is highly confidential. I'm sure you understand. What we are talking about here has never been attempted, so the less we say the better."

Lyra tuned to Jacob. "It's quite all right, Jacob. Demetrius knows I can't give him all the details. But he is a trusted friend." She turned back to Demetrius, her eyes darker and more serious than before.

"It's been hundreds of years since we were forced to leave this planet. Now, Earth has changed. The humans of today are unaware of the supernatural. Their ancestors died off long ago, and with them so did their hatred of our kind. This may be a second chance to blend in and assimilate to their culture."

"But Lyra, they are so different. *We* are so different," Demetrius warned.

"Are we? Where we have magic they have technology," Lyra said. "It will never be perfect, Demetrius, but between you and me, it's best to have a plan in case we can't save the world we live in. If the fighting does begin, then when the smoke clears there will be nothing left of the place we call home."

"So you're saying Earth is the new Haven?"

"No, I'm saying the future that we envisioned thirteen years ago died with Rylan and Alisa Dalcome. I'm saying now is the time to start thinking of a new plan before time runs out and we all end up like the Dalcomes."

CHAPTER 17

The muttering voices came to an abrupt stop as two silver balls of light appeared against the back wall of the living room. The white spheres started out small, no bigger than a softball, but they began to grow larger, sending small flickering currents of electricity, like tentacles, into the air. There was a loud crack followed by two small pops and out of nowhere two women appeared, dressed in long magnificent crimson robes. Sam and Travis jumped, but they seemed to be the only ones startled by their appearance. But it wasn't the oddly dressed women that Sam was concerned with—it was the two large white wolves sitting next to them.

The two wolves were identical. Their coats were pure white, like fresh snow, and their bodies were agile with long slender legs and tapered chests. They moved with a quiet grace, lifting their heads to sniff the stale air. Together they turned toward the two dead bodies. With eyes the color of saffron, they stared at the fallen and Sam felt the skin on his arms prickle. There was something odd about the wolves, something disturbing in the way they looked at the dead. He couldn't quite put his finger on it but it was as if their demeanor was more human than animal.

Sam and Travis exchanged befuddled looks, unsure of what was going on.

"Should I be worried?" Sam asked, turning from the two women and their wolves to Holly. His incredulous look was hard to hide. Holly returned his gaze with faint smile.

"No, Sam, they are just Witches," she said calmly, as if this little bit of information would make Sam feel better.

Sam had to try to keep his mouth from dropping open; the night had gone from terrifying to weird in just a matter of hours.

"Umm, you say that like it's a *good* thing," Travis said nervously. He was sitting bolt upright, and his mouth had fallen open again.

Holly gave Travis an endearing look. "Yes, it's a very good thing," she said.

Travis seemed hard-pressed to believe that. "Well, it didn't turn out so good for Snow White," he muttered.

Sam leaned closer to Holly, still troubled that large white wolves were just a few feet away from them.

"So, why the wolves?" he whispered. He was guessing they were wolves; he really didn't know. Maybe they were huskies—just really *big* huskies.

Still holding Sarah's hand, Travis got to his knees and inched himself toward Sam and Holly. "I've never seen dogs like that, Sam," Travis whispered.

Sam was just about to agree when Holly spoke. "They are called Familiars," she said quietly.

"They're called what?" Sam asked, slowly turning to face Holly.

"Familiars. They serve the witches and wizards by protecting them as they come of age. It's a very old form of magic but still widely practiced today."

"What do you mean, 'come of age?'" Travis asked, leaning closer now as to not be overhead.

"It's when a witch or wizard gets their powers when they are young. From what I understand it's a spiritual bonding that takes place between the witch and the animal.

Travis paused for a moment, taking this in. "Oooh, well, yeah ... I guess that makes sense," he said, as if that was the most logical explanation for the two large wolves sitting in the living room. "But, they don't look all that young, do they?" he added, looking to the two women.

The witches looked similar in that they were dressed alike, but the resemblance stopped there. One was tall and the other was short. The tall witch was extremely thin with leather-like skin, a narrow face, and sharp, angular features. Her nose was long and pointed. Sam thought she resembled a pelican. The other witch was very short and wide. She had a thick round face and wide lips with large, bulbous eyes. The witches stood engrossed in a hushed conversation while observing the damage to the room and the upstairs landing behind them. The white wolves did not seem to be bothered by their surroundings but instead stared directly at Travis and Holly, as if listening to every word being said.

Holly grinned at Travis, "Don't let them hear you say that."

"Too late," a voice boomed from across the room.

The two boys jumped. Travis looked petrified as the tall and rather lanky witch glared in his direction. He turned bright red and looked as if he had swallowed his tongue.

"Now you did it," whispered Holly out of the side of her mouth. "I forgot to mention—the bond between familiar and master is symbiotic. They share almost everything, including sight and sound."

Travis looked over at Holly sheepishly. "Really, well that would have been helpful to know a minute ago."

"Sorry," Holly replied, trying to suppress a grin.

The tall witch stepped forward, reached into her robes, and swiftly retrieved her wand. It was the color of lilac, long, thin and gnarly, like a slender twig. Travis's mouth fell open for a third time and he began to shuffle back against the couch. Sam wasn't sure whom he was most scared of— the witch with the wand, or the large white wolf following her.

"Back, young man, back!" she snapped in a raspy Russian accent, pointing her wand at Travis.

Travis quickly raised his hands in front of his face, scared of what she might do. Sam tensed and he began to stand up, but he stopped when he felt Holly's hand on his shoulder.

"It's okay, Sam. She won't hurt him," she whispered.

The witch stopped just short of Travis and stood next to Sarah's body. "Now, don't move," she barked, waving her wand in his direction. Her tiny eyes were barely visible beneath the wrinkled folds of skin. Sam could make out thin salt-and-pepper eyebrows that almost touched her nose and dark age spots near the corners of her eyes. "Or I'll turn you into a dung beetle, got it?"

Travis nodded imperceptibly with his mouth gaping wide and his eyes bulging. Still pointing her wand at him, the witch looked down at Sarah and her angry frown vanished.

"Oh, my," she gasped. Her eyebrows rose so high that her forehead almost disappeared completely. The witch's once beady eyes were now large and full of concern. Her neck had become stiff and her shoulders rigid as she clutched her robes near her chest. The white wolf sauntered to the witch's side and squatted down next to Sarah's body with a quiet whimper.

Holly and Sam quickly stood and Sam felt his heart leap to his throat. What had the witch seen? Was Sarah worse?

Quickly, the short squatty witch moved across the room, much faster than Sam would have expected, and joined them, her wolf padding alongside her.

"Tosya, is that what I think it is?" the short witch asked, putting her hand to her chest.

Tosya tilted her long bullet-like head and pursed her lips. "I ... yes ... I think so, Sonia," she stammered. Her reply put Sam on edge. Holly had said it was a good thing that the witches were there. But they were looking at his sister like she was a puzzle to be solved, and from the looks of it they were confused on exactly how to do that. If the witches were supposed to make Sam feel better they were failing miserably. Sarah looked dreadful; she was white as a ghost and was barely breathing. Sam wanted more answers but he was trying to be patient. After all, help had arrived. So for now he would wait and give them a chance to do whatever it was they could do as witches.

"I can't see a thing in here," Tosya complained. "Sonia, dear, can I have some light, please?" But there was no answer from the plump witch. Holly and Sam both looked to Sonia, who was still staring intently at Sarah's motionless body.

"Sonia, dear! Some light, please!" Tosya repeated.

Snapping out of her troubled stare, Sonia jumped and her eyes popped open on her puffy round face. "What? Oh yes, yes, sorry."

She quickly stepped back and retrieved an ivory-colored wand from the deep pockets of her robes. Walking as fast as her squat legs could carry her, she began pacing the perimeter of the room, flicking her pudgy hand and sending small dollops of orange and red flames into the air. Her white wolf trotted behind her with its long snout held high. The flames floated in the air like candles without wax as they spaced themselves evenly around the perimeter of the room. Sam and Travis watched as the once dark and gloomy room gradually came to life with a soft buttery glow.

The house was almost unrecognizable now. Sheetrock, wood, wire, and insulation littered the floor. The room was scorched and spattered with pieces of wood and other fragments lodged deep in the walls, like shrapnel from a bomb blast. Sam felt his heartbeat quicken momentarily. The house was in shambles and it looked nothing like the place he had once called home.

Tosya, who was still scrutinizing Sarah, took a knee, closed her eyes, and ran her twisted wand along the length of Sarah's body. Her hand was steady, gliding just inches above Sarah. Sam watched, paralyzed, his eyes glued to the wand as it swept back and forth. He grimaced as the witch began to mutter softly like someone at an eerie séance. When Tosya opened her eyes again, her pupils and irises had vanished, turning her eyes a bone white. The wolf at her side began to growl, its lips pulled into a tight snarl.

Travis glanced nervously at Sam and mouthed, "Magic."

Sam acknowledged Travis with a quick nod of the head, not wanting to draw any attention to himself. The last thing Sam wanted was for Tosya to be mad at him, too.

When Sonia finally returned to the group, she did not return alone. Demetrius, Lyra, and Jacob were with her. Immersed in half-shadows, they stood silhouetted against a backdrop of flickering flames and whispering incantations that reminded Sam of musical verses. Another minute or so passed before Tosya finally lowered her wand and looked up at Demetrius. Her eyes returned to normal but her troubled stare was worse than ever.

"This is a Viper wound, Demetrius. I'm surprised she's not dead." Demetrius's stern glare confirmed the witch's diagnosis.

"Yes, Tosya," he said heavily, "there were two Vipers." His tone was flat but his amber eyes blazed with the same intensity Sam had seen earlier.

"Two! Good heavens!" Tosya cried. She looked at Sonia in disbelief. Sonia walked forward and placed a hand on Tosya's slender shoulder to steady herself. "Demetrius, I think you better tell me what's going on. I mean," she glanced around the room, "it looks like the Great War happened in here!"

"Didn't the Majesty inform you before you left?" asked Holly, raising an eyebrow.

"No!" Tosya exclaimed. Her nostrils were flared now.

"Minister Bogdan notified us personally," Sonia added, "but all he would tell us is that we needed to report to the infirmary at once and that it was an emergency. So we did as he asked, didn't we, Tosya?" She looked to the thin witch for confirmation.

Tosya nodded in agreement. "When we arrived, we were met by an escort of Centurions and we evaporated into the Black Mountains. From there we were led into the mountain itself and to the portal. It was only then that we were told we were needed off-world and, well, here we are. I mean, can you imagine the shock? Off-world? Us? We had no idea an active portal even existed anymore, much less that we would be dealing with Vipers! We all thought they were dead, didn't we? And ..." Her voice trailed off as she looked down at Sarah. "I knew something wasn't right when I saw the remains of young Gordon in the cavern. Dear me, poor boy; never seen anything like it." She put a hand to her wrinkled cheek. "Dark magic, Demetrius, very dark magic."

Sam and Travis shared the same grievous expression. Sam wasn't exactly sure what the witch was talking about but he had heard enough to know that it sounded like very bad news.

"But I knew the moment we saw this young girl," she continued in a dismal tone. "I could sense the evil and torment that her fragile soul is under."

Sam stepped forward, unable to take it any longer. His pulse was racing again. "Will she be all right, can you help her?" he asked.

Tosya looked up at Sam, then turned to Demetrius. "Demetrius, who are these young men and why are they here?"

"Please," Sam persisted, "answer the question. Will she be all right?" He could hear how desperate he sounded but he didn't care. He was scared and terrified of losing the only person he had left in his family.

Tosya's eyes were bulging and she seemed unable to blink. "The infection is spreading," she said curtly. "We need to get her back to the Majesty." Then she turned her attention back to Demetrius. "We'll need to leave—"

"But can you help her?" Sam cried. Tosya reared her head back in surprise. His defiant tone had stunned her, rendering her momentarily speechless. Sam thought her eyes were going to pop out of her head. Apparently she was not used to being addressed like that by anyone.

"Sam," Demetrius cautioned. His stoic tone caught him off guard. Sam's face had gone red and blotchy now. He turned, ready to round on Demetrius, when Tosya abruptly answered.

"No!"

The word hung in the air with such finality that Sam froze. His mouth was still open ready to argue his point to Demetrius, but no words came out. The room fell silent; even the Centurions standing guard glanced over to Tosya when she spoke.

"Wha ... What?" Travis stammered. His injured face was twisted in disbelief. "But, you ... you have magic."

Tosya shifted about and her eyes averted Travis's disappointed gaze. This time when she spoke, it seemed more forthcoming.

"At best, I can slow the venom from spreading, perhaps prolong the inevitable. But you must understand that this venom was forged from the darkest of magic. One for which there is no cure. Not one that can be conjured, anyway."

"What do you mean," Holly interrupted, "'not one that can be conjured?'" She stared intently at the elder witch. "Is there another way?"

Tosya's beak-like face turned a ruby red, making her gaunt features more apparent beneath the hood of her crimson cloak. She looked up hesitantly at Sonia, who narrowed her eyes into a warning stare.

"Demetrius," Lyra said in her regal tone that swiftly captivated the entire group, "it is time. You have no choice. Secrecy cannot help Sarah now."

Demetrius met Lyra's eyes and his quiet confidence seemed to melt away into a vacant stare. Sam could tell by the look on his face that there was an internal struggle going on, but over what he didn't know. Demetrius grudgingly turned and gave Holly a fleeting look before speaking.

"Tosya," he said firmly. "We need your help. If there is a way we can save Sarah ... Dalcome, we need to know."

Tosya blinked, her flushed face slowly turning pale. "What? What did you say?" Her voice had become meek and unsteady. Her eyes moved to Holly, then to Travis, and finally rested on Sam.

"What are you saying, Demetrius?" She looked at Sam as if she were seeing him for the first time. "Is this ..."

"No," Sonia gasped, "it can't be." She too was now staring at Sam. Sam's frustration had suddenly been sidelined. He was becoming extremely uncomfortable now that everyone was looking at him.

Demetrius leaned down with Hollister in one hand and the other on Tosya's shoulder. Tosya turned, confused. Her eyes searched Demetrius's rugged features for any sign of reason beyond the mystifying conclusion she had apparently come to on her own. Sam almost felt sorry for the witch. He knew what it was like to wake up in a world that was much bigger and more frightening than you could have ever imagined.

"This is Sarah Dalcome," Demetrius said ruefully, "the daughter of Rylan and Alisa Dalcome. And this," Demetrius looked to Sam, "is their one and only son, Samuel Dalcome."

Tosya looked back to Sam, flabbergasted, her beady eyes openly staring at him in the dim candlelight. Gradually, Tosya stood, Sonia hesitantly stepped forward, and together they inched their way closer to Sam. Sam, unsure of what they were doing, wanted to back away but reluctantly stood his ground. Tosya slowly lifted her trembling wand until it was level with his face. The lilac-colored wand illuminated his face as they leaned in closer. What they saw next made their mouths drop open and their pupils dilate.

"The eyes!"

CHAPTER 18

Tosya stepped back so fast that she almost trampled Sonia in the process. Her hand was shaking frantically and Sam thought she might drop her wand at any moment.

"Dear Lord! How ... how?" she stammered. Sonia, who had not budged from her spot, looked mesmerized. Her arched brows and wide eyes made her face look longer than normal. Tosya's white wolf circled in front of her, its eerie orange glare bearing down on Sam.

"What? What's wrong?" Sam asked. Why were they reacting that way and what was wrong with his eyes?

"I would know those eyes anywhere," Tosya cried, her voice trembling. "The same as your parents."

"Tosya, please, calm down. Everything is all right," Demetrius said.

"Calm down?" she roared, turning to face him. "Demetrius Lore, I don't get excited anymore. I'm old, so that stopped happening ages ago. When you reach my age you have seen just about everything. But when you bring someone back from the dead, well, I tend to get a little ... unhinged! So, please, bear with me while I take a moment to comprehend just exactly how the child I helped bring into this world has suddenly been resurrected! If. You. Don't. Mind." she said angrily.

"What?" Sam gasped. What did she mean *bring into this world?*

Demetrius's cheeks turned a light pink, making his white beard look more pronounced on his well-defined face. Lyra quickly put her hand to her mouth, trying desperately to suppress a laugh. Holly suddenly became engrossed with the pommel of her staff, trying to avoid Demetrius's stunned face altogether. Travis shook his head and gave Sam a brooding stare, then muttered something about witches and Snow White again.

But Sam was only half paying attention. It frustrated him that everyone in the room knew his mother and her life better than he did. The more the night progressed, the more Sam felt like his mother's memory was fading away, morphing into some stranger he had never met before.

"Tantalizing eyes they had," Sonia uttered, still standing in the same spot, her eyes blank and dreamy.

"Oh, snap out of it!" croaked Tosya as she nudged Sonia in the arm. "Will someone please tell me what is going on?" she continued, placing a hand to her chest and trying to catch her breath. "How is this possible? Where is Alisa? Is she here too?"

"She's dead," Sam said abruptly. Tosya's rambling came to a halt. Her narrowed eyes softened as they met Sam's piercing blue gaze. "My mother's dead," he continued. "She died tonight trying to save my sister and me." His monotone voice seemed distant and disconnected. "She's lying right behind you."

The words made Tosya and Sonia flinch. They looked at one another as if to summon the courage they would need to face the truth. As they turned, their eyes fell to the covered bodies lying on the floor behind them. Tosya placed a hand to her mouth and Sonia squeezed Tosya's arm. For the first time the two witches saw the strands of long brown hair exposed near the edge of the blanket.

Tosya opened her mouth to speak but then closed it as Sam continued. "That's why it's so important that you answer Holly's question. Is there another way to cure my sister?" He took a step closer, his imploring gaze meeting Tosya's heartfelt eyes. "She is the only family I have left and I need your help to save her." Tosya's eyes began to fill with tears. "Please, I can't lose her too. Please, Tosya."

Tosya's stare wavered under Sam's persistent stare, and her bottom lip quivered as she spoke. "I ... I can—"

"Please," Sam insisted, not giving her a chance to reply, "help me."

He knew he seemed relentless in his pursuit for an answer, but this was his sister he was talking about and if there was a way to save Sarah he was going to find it.

"You don't understand, Samuel," Sonia whispered. Her voice sounded frightened and feeble.

"What?" he asked. "What don't I understand? Tell me."

"The quest is far too dangerous," she said, looking to Sarah. "To venture down this road would be madness. The journey alone could kill you."

"Tosya, please. You've said enough," Sonia said softly. "Think of Alisa ... what Alisa would have wanted."

"My mom would want me to save my sister," Sam said

sharply. He was looking at Sonia when he spoke but she would not meet his gaze. Frustrated, he turned back to Tosya, determined to make his point. "Please, Tosya, tell me what you know. Tell me how I can help her, how I can save Sarah."

A single tear traveled the length of Tosya's withered cheek as she looked up at Sam. "The Elixir of Life," she finally confessed. Sam could not help but notice the tone of despair in her trembling voice. Her will to fight had suddenly vanished the moment she'd seen his mother's body.

"Tosya, no," Sonia groaned.

Demetrius and Holly exchanged worried looks, but it was Lyra who spoke first.

"But that's just a myth, an old wives' tale," she said suspiciously as a small frown line appeared on her forehead.

"No," Tosya said softly, "the truth becomes a myth when death robs it of its proof."

Travis raised an eyebrow and looked over at Sam. "Um, that sounds ... bad."

"The journey would be very treacherous. You could not do it alone."

"He would not be alone," Holly added quickly as she moved closer to Sam. Her face was burning with a defiant glare.

Sam felt warmed by Holly's gesture. He would need her help but he was fully prepared to do it alone if that's what it took. He gave Holly a tight smile but she didn't see him. Her eyes had not moved from Tosya.

Suddenly there was a flash and Vallen reappeared behind them in a haze of blue mist. "So, where exactly is this Elixir of Life?" he asked smugly.

Everyone turned to look at Vallen. Lyra glared and shook her head, annoyed at his flamboyant entrance. It was obvious that he had been listening upstairs the entire time. But by the look on his arrogant face, he didn't care what anyone thought about his intrusion.

"It's not *where*," Sonia said coldly. "The Elixir is not something to be had, it's something to be created."

Demetrius and Holly exchanged bewildered looks. Lyra and Jacob said nothing but stared blankly at Sonia. Travis squinted and scratched his head; Vallen just looked aggravated now. Sam glanced around the room and felt relieved. For the first time everyone seemed to be just as confused as he was.

"What do you mean, Sonia?" Demetrius asked, his amber eyes bright with intrigue.

Sonia did not speak right away. Her lips were pursed and her posture became rigid as she contemplated her answer.

"The Elixir of Life has many ingredients, but only one rare component. Extremely rare." Her cold stare did not falter when she looked into his eyes.

He returned her gaze and asked calmly, "And what is that?"

"Abyon," Tosya said flatly as she fidgeted with her wand, spinning it between her thumb and forefinger.

Sonia sighed. "Well, now you've gone and done it," she said. All her attempts at being stubborn and intimidating had vanished. "You're going to get them all killed!"

As if she had been awakened from a trance, Tosya turned and glared at Sonia. Her white wolf stood at attention.

"He has a right to know and I will not take that from him!" she said, almost yelling now. "And the boy is right.

Alisa would have wanted him to save his sister, to do whatever it takes, because she was a fighter and so is the boy. He's a Dalcome for God's sake!"

Tosya stood and abruptly stowed her wand in her pocket. Then she straightened her robes, indicating nothing more was to be said on that matter.

Sam felt a wave a vindication sweep through him and he almost smiled. But he couldn't help but wonder who his mother and father were in this world they called Haven. He wasn't stupid. He had pieced it together. His mother knew magic, she knew Holly—the letter in her Quarrem had proven that. Demetrius and possibly Vallen were her friends as well, all from another life that she was trying so desperately to protect him from. A life she had shared with his father before he and his sister were born. But why leave? What had happened that made them run from the only place they called home? Sam didn't know all the answers, but it was starting to come together and soon he would have them all.

"Isn't Abyon a tree?" Lyra asked. She looked puzzled as she stepped closer to Tosya.

"It's a one-of-a-kind tree, from what I've heard," Vallen said.

"Yes, that is correct," Tosya said sharply, still a little agitated. "There were not many to begin with, but now they are virtually extinct. Only one Abyon tree exists today."

"Where?" Demetrius asked, his interest piqued now. It sounded like he wanted to know as much as Sam did, which made Sam feel a little better about him. If Demetrius was a friend of his mother's, then he would know saving Sarah is what she would have wanted.

Tosya's eyes became heavy and her jaw drooped, as if she was recalling something very unpleasant. "In the valley of Shadowfay," she said in a vacant tone.

There were shared looks of concern upon hearing this. Sam was feeling more uncomfortable by the moment. This was obviously not good news. Wherever this Shadow place was, no one seemed too eager to get there.

"The Valley of Bones," Lyra muttered under her breath, her green eyes dark and distant.

Travis leaned over to Sam and whispered in his ear, "And that sounds real bad."

"Yeah," Sam moaned, looking disappointed.

"In the Valley of Shadowfay is a mountain. Inside that mountain grows the Abyon," Tosya continued. Her eyes moved to Demetrius. "It is the seed of the Abyon that you must procure for the Elixir of Life."

"That's it? A seed?" Vallen scoffed. "We're looking for a seed?"

"Vallen, let her finish," Demetrius objected.

Vallen threw his hands in the air and rolled his eyes. "Fine."

Tosya looked to Demetrius, who gestured for her to continue. "There is a reason why the Abyon is so rare. A single seed of the ancient tree drops once every thirty years and dies within a year if it does not take root," she said.

Sonia looked to Sam. She placed her stubby hand on her round chin and began shaking her head, which made Sam feel even worse. The room filled with heavy sighs and Demetrius put a hand to his forehead.

"The odds of you finding a seed are infinitesimal, Samuel, much less finding it alive. Not to mention you would have to survive the journey through Shadowfay and into the mountain where the Fay live. No one has ever done that before."

Sam's heart sank. Just like that, their only hope had been snuffed out. He looked away to the floating flames that danced against the back wall of the house and then down to his mother's covered body. *What would you do, Mom?* he wondered.

But he knew the answer to that question. She would go. She would take the journey and never look back. She would do anything for her children. Sam took in a deep breath, straightened himself up and looked straight into Sonia's eyes.

"When do we leave?"

CHAPTER 19

Sonia looked like she had been slapped in the face. Her round fluffy cheeks had turned red and her giant yellow eyes were so big that she reminded Sam of a toad.

"Wha ... what?" Sonia stammered. "But ... but you can't!"

"I'm with the kid," bellowed Vallen from behind the group. He tilted his staff in Sam's direction and a pompous smirk spread across his face.

Sonia looked beside herself. Her head twitched back and forth between Sam and Vallen, and small curls of red hair began to fall from beneath her hood into her eyes. She looked to Demetrius in desperation.

"Demetrius, talk some sense into the child. This is too dangerous. He won't survive."

"You mean *we*, don't you?" Holly interjected.

Another curl fell into Sonia's face. "Demetrius, please!"

All eyes were on Demetrius; even the two white wolves were staring at the Master Keeper. Demetrius looked to be in serious thought, his amber eyes shifting between Sam and Travis, as if he was contemplating the risk of bringing them, or perhaps of taking the journey at all.

Without a word, Demetrius tapped Hollister's pommel and the emerald gemstone ignited into a dazzling green flame. A piece of faded parchment appeared within the fire.

"Bellisoria, circumstances have changed," he said as a smaller dark flame of yellow and purple burst onto the parchment and began to scribe his words. "I will not be returning to the Majesty. I will be taking the Dalcome boy to Ashaway Cottage. I will send you a scroll once I've arrived. There is much to discuss."

There was a pause as the flaming parchment rolled itself into a tight scroll and disappeared into the emerald flame. Demetrius held Hollister by its shaft and waved his free hand dismissively through the flame. The flame vanished.

"Amazing!" Jacob gasped. All heads turned; everyone seemed to have forgotten Jacob, who had been standing behind Lyra quietly observing.

"Demetrius, no!" Sonia pleaded, "You can't do this."

"Enough!" Tosya said, glowering at Sonia. "We are here to give aid to the wounded and prepare the deceased for transport." Her tone was absolute. "I suggest we get back on task, Miss Yazov, if you don't mind!"

Calling Sonia by her last name seemed to jolt her into action. Her frustrated scowl slackened and with a heavy sigh she turned and walked toward Xavier's covered body.

But Tosya wasn't done yet. Her glare cut to Demetrius. "I know I'm just a healer, Demetrius, and my opinion counts for little, but the path you have chosen is extremely dangerous." Demetrius opened his mouth to speak but Tosya held up her hand, to silence him. "Let an old witch have her say, will you?" Demetrius closed his mouth in a flat expression. "We just got the boy back after all these years. Don't go getting him killed. Some chapters may have come to an end tonight," her gaze fell to Alisa's body and she let out a small moan, "but the boy is a new beginning." She looked back up at Demetrius. "Keep him safe," she said softly, her golden eyes bright with emotion. Then she turned without giving Demetrius a chance to respond and joined Sonia by Xavier's body.

Demetrius said nothing. He stared at the spot where Tosya had stood. Holly, Lyra, and Jacob also seemed to be lost in thought.

Sam felt he should say something, something inspiring and uplifting—after all, he was the one that pressed the issue about Shadowfay. But who was he kidding? He couldn't even argue with his sister without sounding like a complete moron, much less try to lift spirits. With his luck he would probably make someone cry; he was good at that.

Sam looked over at Travis, who was rubbing his wrists, captivated by the two witches preparing the bodies for their journey home. Tosya and Sonia moved next to Xavier and Alisa and pulled back the blankets, exposing their pale expressionless faces. The two Keepers looked at peace with their eyes closed. Maybe they were at peace, Sam thought. Tosya and Sonia lifted their wands and made a single sweeping motion over each body followed by three subtle swishes, first at the head, then the chest, and finally at the feet. Black ash materialized and fell like snow, gathering just inches above the bodies, as if it were falling on a flat, invisible surface.

Sam stood motionless, clenching his jaw. It pained him to think this might be the last time he would ever see his mother's face, but if it was then this was how he would remember her—with no signs of worry or fatigue from being overworked, but at peace because finally she found the serenity she had been searching for on Earth. He would miss her dearly, but above all he would miss the way she made him feel—warm and comforted, the way a mother should. He could feel the emotion swelling inside of him again and he took in a long, measured breath to calm himself.

"Goodbye, Mom," he whispered quietly. "I love you."

Within minutes, the bodies were consumed in a blanket of ash. The witches stepped forward and touched the tips of their wands to the center of the black mass and there was a faint crackling sound as the ash solidified. The decorative lines and angles of two coffins began to materialize as the once powdery texture crystalized, turning from black ash to a gleaming onyx finish.

The entire room watched as the witches moved their wands in swift circles, levitating the coffins several inches off the ground. Tosya then moved across the room to Sarah, making tight swirls above Sarah's body with her wand, and within seconds she too began to levitate. Without thinking, Travis took a step forward. He looked as if he wanted to stop Tosya, but he stood his ground.

"Where are they taking her?" Sam asked to no one in particular.

"To the infirmary at the Majesty," Holly said as she placed a hand on Sam's shoulder. "She will be safe there."

Sam watched as Sarah's body hovered in front of Tosya, unaware of where she was headed. His throat felt tight as he swallowed. It was hard for him to see his sister so vulnerable.

Sarah had always been strong and vibrant and now she looked small and fragile. There were a lot of things he could never tell her because they didn't have that kind of relationship. But now, if he had the chance to do it all over again, things would be different. He would tell his sister that she was courageous and that he was proud of her. She might tell him he was being a dork and then ask if he was on drugs, or perhaps agree with him whole-heartedly. But he didn't care because right now, at this moment, he would give anything just to hear her voice again. Sam straightened himself up and tried to suppress the emptiness he felt at seeing Sarah leave.

Tosya and Sonia moved with the two coffins, Sarah, and their white wolves to the back wall. The group stepped closer to the witches, leaving the Centurion standing guard in the center of the room.

"Well then," Tosya said, "it's time." Her eyes were bright with age in the candlelight and her face was lined with experience and wisdom. "I'm truly sorry about your mother, Samuel. She was one of the bravest, most talented people I've ever known. Both of your parents were."

Sam could hear the pain in her voice as if it physically hurt her to talk about it anymore. He wasn't sure what to say. He never knew his father and he never knew this person his mother was supposed to have been. He knew her as the overworked, underpaid waitress trying to raise two kids as a single parent. That was the person he knew, not this leader, this magical warrior from another world. With his mind drawing a blank, Sam resorted to "Thank you," and forced a smile.

Tosya reached up with her frail arm and placed a hand to Sam's cheek, taking him by surprise. "I really did help bring you into this world," she said softly. "I was the one who delivered both you and your sister."

Sam's eyes grew wider, "Really?"

"Oh, yes. You were such pretty babies, too. Those eyes, those magnificent blue eyes. I would have recognized them anywhere," she said dreamily, her voice trailing off.

Sam smiled shyly but his mind was churning out questions so fast he could barely contain himself. He wanted to know about his past. He wanted to know what his parents were like when they had been happy. He wanted to hear about their lives and the things they did and shared with one another when they were a family. But he said nothing and his smile faded as he forced himself to remain quiet.

Tosya then turned to Travis and a smirk crept across her face.

"You had a bit of a go at it, didn't you?" she asked.

Travis's raised his eyebrows, confused. He looked to Sam, but Sam shrugged his shoulders.

"Your face," she snapped, and she lifted her wand to his forehead and gave it a stern tap. There was a loud crack.

"Ouch!" Travis screeched. He jerked his hands to his face and rubbed his head.

"There, that should do it," she said, happy with herself.

"What was that for?" he groaned, pulling his hands down and glaring at her.

But the dark blue and yellow bruises around Travis's eyes had vanished. His nose was no longer swollen or broken. He looked just like he had before, before the encounter with the Viper.

"Your face," Sam said, stepping in front of Travis to take a better look.

Travis turned grim. "What? What's wrong with it?" he asked, patting his cheeks, nose and forehead.

"Nothing. It looks, well, normal," Sam mused.

"What?" Travis gasped, continuing to pat his face.

Tosya looked back to Sam, who only had a few minor cuts and scrapes and lifted her wand again.

Sam held up a hand. "No, really, I'm fine. Thanks though," he said cheerfully.

She smiled and looked to Holly and Demetrius.

"Take care of them."

Demetrius stepped next to Holly. "We will. Be safe."

Tosya tried to smile, but her concern kept her from seeming sincere. She turned to Lyra and bowed. "Princess Lyra."

Lyra bowed her head slightly. *Princess,* Sam thought. He and Travis stared at Lyra as she kept her gaze on Tosya and Sonia. But Sam felt she knew they were staring at her.

Tosya stepped back with Sonia, Sarah, the two white wolves, and the onyx coffins. Sonia gave a tender wave and with a flash of white light they turned into seven silver spheres of electricity and vanished with a resounding pop.

"Amazing," Jacob said, for the third time that night.

They all stared at the empty spot for several minutes, each person consumed in their own thoughts. Sam was feeling tired; the night was finally catching up with him but he knew there was still more to do. And part of him was relieved that Sarah would be in good hands until they could find the Elixir of Life.

"Now what, Demetrius?" Sam asked.

"Now we wait for Coppertop."

"What's a Coppertop," Travis asked, sitting down on the arm of the couch.

"Not a what, but a who," Demetrius corrected. "He works for the Majesty, in Magical Sterilization. He's the best. A bit odd," Demetrius smirked, "but good."

"But what does Coppertop do exactly?" Travis asked.

"He will cleanse all traces of magic from the house. He will also place the house back in order, back to its original condition. Once we leave there will be no sign of magic or any evidence that this night even occurred."

Sam wished it were that easy. He wished they could perform some kind of magic that could just turn back time, erase the night completely as if it had never happened. He would give anything to hear his mother's voice now, or even to see Sarah's notorious grin. He closed his eyes and winced, placing a hand to his head. He could feel it throbbing behind his eyes. It was either from sleep deprivation or stress. There were hours, maybe minutes before he took a journey that might end his life. Being back at school, playing dodgeball, and being harassed by Daniel Harris didn't seem so bad now.

"Are you okay, Sam?" Holly asked, watching him rub his eyes.

"I'm fine," he said, and gave a small shrug. "Just a headache."

"See, you should have had the witch slap you in the face with the wand. You'd feel like a million bucks now," Travis said, grinning.

"Yeah, maybe," Sam said, pulling his hand away and straightening himself up.

"Hey, Demetrius," Travis said, addressing him like they were old friends, "how come there are no police here?"

Demetrius looked to Holly, obviously confused, but Holly looked just as bewildered. Together they looked to Vallen.

"What?" Vallen asked. "I have no idea what a police is."

"Yes, that's a very good question," Jacob said, nodding his head in agreement. "Why is it no one heard the ruckus, I mean," he looked to the upstairs landing where the three Centurions were standing guard, "it looks as if a bomb went off in here."

"Yeah," Travis added, "exactly my point. Why is it that you two," he pointed to Lyra and Jacob, "showed up and no one else did?"

"It was because of the Viper's Binding spell," Lyra explained.

"The what?" Jacob asked, titling his head to one side.

"It's a powerful containment spell. Not only will it imprison the victim from coming and going, but it will also contain any sound or air within the radius of the spell."

"Oh," Travis murmured, "kind of like a bubble?"

"Um, yes, kind of like that," Lyra frowned.

Sam put his hand to his head again and ran his hand through his thick black hair, trying not to make it obvious that his head was still hurting. But Holly noticed it at once.

"Sam, why don't we go sit down until Coppertop arrives."

Sam nodded and walked to the couch. Travis slid off the arm of the sofa and onto the cushion and they sat together in silence.

Holly looked down at the boys as they stared blankly ahead. They looked drained, with dark circles underneath their eyes, unkempt hair, and tattered clothes. The boys had fought for their lives tonight and they looked like it. She turned her attention to Demetrius and he nodded. Holly bit her lip and sighed.

"Sam," she said. Sam looked up to see the troubled look on her face. "I will be leaving soon," she continued, looking down at her boots.

"What?" he asked. "What do you mean? I thought ..."

"Oh, I will be joining you on the journey to Shadowfay," she said quickly. "Vallen and I need to return to the Majesty, but we will join you as soon as we can."

"But why? I ... I don't understand," he said. "And what is the Majesty anyway?"

Holly leaned against her staff. "The Majesty is much like your government here. I believe that is the correct terminology," she said, frowning. "Sorry, it's been awhile. The leader of the Majesty is a witch named Bellisoria. She is the one responsible for finding and establishing Haven's society. Demetrius, Vallen, and I are part of the Majesty. It's our duty to protect the interests of the Majesty. Right now we need to report back to inform them of what took place here and what has happened to your mother, sister, and Xavier. But once that is done, and once Demetrius has ironed out a solid plan for Shadowfay, I will join you again. I promise."

Holly knelt down next to Sam, placed her staff on the floor by his feet, and slowly reached for his hand. She stared for a moment at their hands and looked up slowly. Her majestic eyes searched Sam's face as if to take in every feature, as if she might not see him again. In that moment of silence Sam felt the emptiness inside himself stirring, wanting to resurface, wanting to mix with his emotions and manipulate his thoughts. The walls of acceptance he had built up over the last few hours fell under attack by the despair and loneliness that were lingering just outside the gate. He knew he could not allow that to happen; he could not allow his emotions to control him. Now more than ever, he would have to count on himself to stay strong. It was no longer just about himself—it was about his sister and keeping her alive.

Holly finally spoke with a tenderness in her voice. "You know, I have waited a long time to meet you, Samuel Dalcome." She held out her other hand with an impish smile. "I am Hollerin Quinn, but my friends call me Holly."

Sam and Travis both smiled. Sam took her hand and together they shook. Holly then turned, "Travis."

Still smiling, Travis held out his hand. "Travis Martin, but you can call me Trav."

Holly grinned. "Okay, Trav."

She turned back to Sam and her expression stiffened. "I am sorry the circumstances could not be better. Your mother was a wonderful person and an honored Keeper. I am proud to have called her my friend. We all are." As Holly said this, she was joined by Demetrius, Vallen, and Lyra. Jacob had remained behind to give them some privacy.

"Samuel, I know everything is happening very fast. You must have a thousand questions and I promise they will all be answered in due time. But right now I need you to trust me that we are your friends and we are here to help," she said as she stared into his eyes. "Can you do that?" She squeezed his hand again.

Sam might have said no if it weren't for the letter he had seen from Holly to his mother. Not to mention they had all risked their lives for his family tonight and were probably the only people that could help his sister now.

"I read the letter about the spell." Sam knew that came out all wrong. He could tell by the look on her furrowed brow.

"The spell?" she said softly.

"Yes," he replied. "Narravista."

As soon as the word left his mouth the debris next to him began to creek and shudder. Slowly, fragments of furniture and other wreckage began to levitate in the air. Holly looked from side to side, tightening her grip on Sam, craning her neck back to get a better look at the objects that were now hovering several feet from the ground.

Sam looked around sheepishly. It was happening again. He looked at Holly and was surprised to see a slow, incredulous smile spread across her face. He glanced up at Demetrius and Vallen, who were also staring at the floating debris.

"Well, you are just full of surprises aren't you, Samuel?" Demetrius said calmly.

"Extraordinary," Lyra muttered looking at Vallen, who grimaced.

Travis, on the other hand, was not so impressed. His body had gone tense. He remembered what had happened the last time Sam had used that word, and the objects floating now were much bigger than a baseball.

"Sam, what are you doing?" he asked, his voice a little unsteady. "I thought we weren't going to use that word anymore."

"I'm sorry, I ... didn't mean too ... Narravista!" Sam said quickly.

Everything came crashing down at once. Sam and Travis

closed their eyes and cringed until everything had settled. Sam heard the sound of breaking glass and a loud yelp from Jacob in the background. "I'm okay," he hollered. "I'm ... fine, just caught me off guard."

Sam opened one eye at a time to see Holly beaming.

"Sorry about that," he said reluctantly. "That happens every time I say that word. I don't know why, it just does," he looked down to the ground, embarrassed.

Holly cleared her voice and took Sam's chin, lifting his head so she could see his eyes.

"There is no need to apologize, Sam, it's who you are. It's who we are," she said calmly as her eyes met his.

"Who *I* am," Sam repeated. He wasn't sure if he was asking a question or making a statement. He didn't feel sure of anything anymore. Was he like them? Like his mother? Did Sarah have the same abilities too? He remembered his mother telling her that she must suppress her fear, that she needed to remain calm; that being calm places you in control. But he had no idea what she meant.

"Sam," Holly said, breaking him from his train of thought. She looked over at Demetrius again but Demetrius never moved or said a word. Holly turned to look back at Sam again and pursed her lips. "Well, never mind. All in good time. There will be plenty of time for all of that."

"Holly, it's time," Vallen said.

Holly did not respond but continued to stare at Sam. "You have a gift Sam, one that you cannot possibly imagine, and in time you will come to understand all of this, I promise. But for now you will have to go on blind faith and trust what your heart is telling you, okay?"

Sam looked at her, unsure of what to say. He didn't want her to leave. He trusted her and there was not much he felt he could trust in this world anymore. But Holly had promised she would be back and if he trusted her, it would have to be enough.

"Yes," he said hesitantly.

"Good," she said, smiling. "Good"

"So, where am *I* going?" he asked, his eyes now searching her face for the answer.

"You will be going with Demetrius. He's a Keeper like me, but he is a very powerful Keeper. There is none better, nor wiser" she said with a wink.

Holly placed her other hand on top on Sam's. It was then that Sam noticed her ring; it was the same ring with the red ruby that he had found in his mother's Quarrem. The same ring that belonged to his father.

"Be strong, young Samuel." She squeezed his hand one last time, then reached for her staff before standing and returning to Vallen's side.

"I'm ready" she told Demetrius.

"Very well, I'll contact you when we're settled in," Demetrius said.

Holly looked back at Sam and gave him one last smile before turning to walk into the foyer with Vallen. They stood next to one another in their long cloaks, tall boots, and gray armor. Sam thought they looked intimidating but no longer out of the scope of reality—not his reality anyway. His perception of what was possible had been changed forever. It had changed the night Xavier walked into his life. Looking straight ahead, the two Keepers raised their staffs simultaneously and brought them to the ground. Flashes of purple and blue light engulfed their bodies, leaving only a trace of a fine mist in their wake. Sam stared into the empty space, his eyes following the last remnants of the purple and blue haze as it swayed in the air before finally disappearing.

Chapter 20

"Demetrius, it's time," Lyra said. "Jacob and I should be leaving as well. I'm sure Coppertop will be here any moment and well, no offense, but I would rather not be here when he arrives."

Sam and Travis peered at one another from the corners of their eyes.

Demetrius raised an eyebrow and nodded in agreement. "None taken—I completely understand."

Lyra looked down at Sam. "Unpleasant man, long story," she said, rolling her eyes. Sam gave a fait smile and nodded his head as if he understood. He didn't really understand but he didn't know what else to do. He and Travis both stood and Lyra placed a hand on his shoulder.

"I wish you the best, Sam, I truly do. I know if there is anyone who can help you save your sister it is Demetrius." She looked at Demetrius and smiled. "He's not an elf, mind you, but as far as Keepers go, there really is none better. You're in good hands." Demetrius shook his head, slightly embarrassed.

"Sam, Travis," Jacob said hurriedly, "best of luck. Be safe." Sam and Travis took turns shaking his hand. Jacob seemed eager to leave—the man had been on edge since he had walked into the house, but with good reason, Sam thought.

Lyra finally turned to Demetrius, her emerald eyes aglow and her smile gleaming white. "Again, it was really good to see you, Demetrius. I wish it could have been under better circumstances."

"As do I," Demetrius said, smiling back. "Will you be returning to Haven?"

"I'm not sure. Perhaps in a few months unless I hear otherwise. There is a lot Jacob and I need to attend to, but who knows, after what happened here? There is no telling what effect this will have on the Majesty and its constituents."

Demetrius glanced at Sam and Travis, who were both listening but not looking in his direction. But Sam's flushed face and red ears were a dead giveaway, and Travis fiddling with his shirt didn't help either.

"Come, I'll walk you out," Demetrius said.

Lyra smiled at the two boys one last time as she, Jacob, and Demetrius made their way to the front door.

"Dude," Travis said under his breath, "I wonder what she meant by that?"

"Not sure," Sam said, "but I'm thinking that's the least of our problems now."

Travis turned to Sam, nodded, and pursed his lips. "Yeah."

As Demetrius said his final goodbyes and turned back to Sam and Travis, Sam noticed a small white sphere appear by the crumpled staircase. Just like before, the small ball of light began to grow, sending out thin tentacles of light into the dimly lit room. A crack rang out followed by a small pop and there, standing amongst the debris, was a tall wiry man with a scrawny black cat perched on his shoulder.

Dressed in a frayed burgundy vest, a pea green shirt, and tattered black pants, he hobbled into the light. His head was mostly bald except for patches of fuzzy gray hair that protruded from the sides so that it looked like the stuffing was coming out of his head. He had one bushy gray eyebrow that ran the width of his withered, pale forehead. His deep-set eyes were a muddy brown color and he had dark liver spots near the corners of his mouth and on the sides of his cheeks. The more Sam looked at the man, the more he thought he resembled a clown without all the elaborate makeup.

"Wow, does Dirty Ernie have a brother?" Travis whispered.

"No kidding," Sam groaned. He stared at the odd man who was looking around at his new surroundings like he was disgusted at what he saw. He sniffed the air and wrinkled his flat, crooked nose like he smelled something foul. He was frowning so hard that his one eyebrow was touching the bridge of his nose.

"Yes, Poppy, in shambles, always in shambles," he croaked, turning to the cat who was now staring at Sam and Travis. Sam did a double take when he saw the cat's eyes. They were the same eerie saffron color as the white wolves'.

"The cat's eyes look familiar," Sam whispered.

"Yeah, creepy familiar," Travis replied.

Coppertop scanned the room until he caught sight of Demetrius. His scowling face slowly curled into a malicious grin, revealing teeth the color of mold.

"Lore," he grunted. "I might have known. Made a mess of things, have you?"

Demetrius stepped forward with his staff in one hand. "Hello, Coppertop, how nice to see you again." His voice was so flat that it sounded like he was falling asleep.

Coppertop's grin slowly faded back into a look of disgust. "Yes, I'm sure it is. Enough with the pleasantries, Lore." He waved his hand dismissively, startling the black cat, which moved across his back to his other shoulder. "You know I'm a busy man. What have you done now? Fill me in. What's the damage and who are your friends there?" He pointed a long dirty finger in Sam's and Travis's direction. "You know the rules, Lore—no witnesses. I don't like an audience," he said in a raspy English accent. He wheezed after each sentence to catch his breath as if it might be his last.

Demetrius ignored the man's line of questioning and went straight into the introductions. "Samuel, Travis, this is Everest Coppertop. He is from the department of Magical Sterilization. He is the one we have been waiting on for so long." The snide comment did not go unnoticed by Coppertop, who chewed on his bottom lip and grumbled something underneath his breath. Poppy the cat hissed in Demetrius's direction, mimicking her master's frustration.

"Coppertop, meet Samuel Dalcome and his friend, Travis ..."

"Martin. Travis Martin," Travis said timidly.

"Yes, Travis Martin," Demetrius added.

Coppertop narrowed his eyes and scratched his pointed chin with a long yellow fingernail, making his dangling jowls wiggle. It looked like he was using every last brain cell to comprehend what he had just heard.

"Daaaalcome," he sneered. The name rolled off his tongue like it tasted awful to say. "Rylan and Alisa's child?"

Travis nudged Sam. "Man, you must be really popular over there."

Sam nudged Travis back. "Shut up."

Demetrius looked back at Sam and gave him a quick wink. "Yes, that would be the one."

"Well, well, what do you know? Those old gypsies at the Lazy Lizard were telling the truth. You know, I never believed a word those old bats said, much less anyone else at that Tavern. All a bunch of drunken fairies they are. But here you be ... a living, breathing Dalcome." Poppy hissed again and Coppertop wiped his nose with the back of his hand. "I heard stories about you, boy, but I thought it was just hearsay, myths, or flat-out lies." Coppertop's gaze cut to Demetrius. "I also heard there were two. What of the other, Lore? Is there another child?"

"Yes," Sam snapped. He had already made up his mind—he didn't like Coppertop or his cat. "I have a sister."

"Ssssister" Coppertop hissed, looking back at Sam. His eyes were wider now, his interested piqued. "Where is she, boy? Where is this sister you speak of?"

"She—" Sam began.

"She is safe, Coppertop," Demetrius interrupted. "Please, don't let us keep you from your work. I am quite sure you have plenty to do."

Coppertop's shifty eyes moved from Sam to Demetrius. He was scowling now, which caused his bushy eyebrow to obscure his dark eyes. "Yes, well ... I will need you to leave then, wont I?" he growled, his stained teeth reappearing in an unpleasant sneer.

"Poppy, off, off you go, and stay close. Daddy has work to do."

The black cat leapt from Coppertop's shoulder and landed gracefully on the ground next to him. Her bottle-brush tail wrapped whimsically around his leg as she circled beneath him. Coppertop looked around the house again in utter disgust, and he gave a slight jolt, like he had been slapped in the back of the head. His eyes grew wide and his thin, cracked lips curled into a greedy grin as he noticed the Vipers on the floor.

"And there they are," he said, brimming with delight. He made his way across the room until he was standing dead center between the remains of the two beasts.

"Yes, a bit of bad business here," he said in a surly tone. "I see the gypsies were right about you buggers, too." Poppy, who had lagged behind Coppertop, eased her way between his bowed legs and craned her neck to sniff the Vipers' corpses. Her nose began to twitch the closer she came to the Viper's hands. She was there only seconds before she sprang back, her tail up and body arched. Coppertop looked down, startled, as the cat hissed and ran behind the broken coffee table. "Yes, Poppy, a bit of bad business," he sneered as he reached into his vest pocket and withdrew his wand. "Always a mess, always," he mumbled to himself as he stepped over the Vipers' bodies. "And what do we have here?"

Sam watched as the creepy old man moved his wand closer to the Viper's sword lying on the ground.

"A new relic for the Majesty, I think," he said as he touched the tip of his wand to the ominous black blade. As soon as it touched the blade, Coppertop's wand began to glow like a hot ember, sending silver ribbons of smoke swirling into the air.

"Great goblins!" Coppertop cried as he jumped back, shaking his wand in the air. The wand became brighter and the smoke darker the faster he moved it through the air.

Both boys began to smile. *Serves him right,* Sam thought.

Travis could barely contain himself as he leaned over to Sam. "Welcome to the nightmare, pal," he whispered.

Coppertop hopped and skipped about, waving his wand around until the bright orange glow was finally extinguished.

Breathing hard, he turned with a sneer just in time to catch a glimpse of Demetrius's broad grin.

"You!" Coppertop roared, pointing his long gnarly finger in Demetrius's direction. "You knew that was going to happen, didn't you?"

Demetrius had momentarily managed to stifle his grin. "But of course not," he said calmly.

Coppertop's eyes launched daggers at Demetrius as he moved the tip of his wand to his mouth and blew on it, sending tendrils of black smoke into the air again.

"I will need you to make the sword ready for transport, and the staff too." Demetrius pointed to Nara, who was lying on the kitchen counter next to the Quarrem and the rucksack. "They will be coming with me."

Sam's smile faded and his heart felt like it had stopped beating when he saw Nara lying there, her sapphire gemstone dark and forsaken as if she too was dead. He was relieved that Demetrius was taking the staff with them. It was one of the few things he had left that had meant something to his mother. Besides, Sarah would kill him if he left it behind.

Coppertop's murky eyes tripled in size and his lips began to quiver. Sam thought the old man was having a heart attack.

"What? But you can't, that's a magic item. It should be sent to the Majesty as part of the evidence of sterilization."

Sam looked to Demetrius. His casual demeanor was gone, leaving only a cold, desolate glare on his face.

"I wasn't asking, Coppertop," Demetrius warned. Sam and Travis did not budge, but glanced at one another nervously.

"But—" Coppertop said with a gulp.

"Mahan," Demetrius called to the Centurion standing in the room with them, "I need you to help Mr. Coppertop here. Please ensure everything is packed to my specifications. Can you do that for me, soldier?"

Sam and Travis looked at the Centurion, who towered above them. The soldier turned his menacing winged helmet in Coppertop's direction. "With pleasure, sir," he said in a deep, gruff voice. Coppertop's head shook nervously as he peered at the Centurion from the corner of his eye.

Demetrius looked down at Sam with a derisive smile. "Yes, quite charming isn't he?" And just like that Demetrius's calm demeanor had returned and Sam couldn't help but smile back.

"Yeah, quite," he said.

"I think I liked Dirty Ernie better," Travis said, elbowing Sam in the arm. "At least Ernie never talked."

Sam nodded, "Good point."

Demetrius began to walk toward where the stairs used to be. "Let's give Coppertop some room, shall we? Believe it or not he is quite good at his job," he said, looking up at the Centurions standing guard upstairs. Their sapphire staffs illuminated the top floor, bathing the walls in a radiant blue glow.

"Come, we will need to gather your belongings for the journey," Demetrius said.

Sam guessed he would be taking only what he could carry, which was fine by him. He was pretty sure they didn't have any Sony PlayStations where he was going, so just the essentials would have to do.

Without saying a word, Demetrius moved Hollister between the three of them and Sam grabbed the black and silver staff. Travis looked apprehensive but grabbed Hollister with a firm grasp, as if his very life depended on it.

"Ready?" Demetrius asked. Sam nodded. Travis twitched his head like he was having a mild spasm in his neck. Demetrius gripped the staff firmly and tapped Hollister once on the ground and everything went dark again. Sam watched as the room vanished, swallowed up by the green flash of light from Demetrius's staff. He felt like he was falling and his stomach lurched, making him grimace with nausea. A wave of crushing pressure moved over his body, causing his skin to ripple. It felt like he was on the fastest roller coaster ride of his life. Then, just like before, a sliver of green light appeared in the distance. Sam closed his eyes as he sped toward the light, knowing that it was almost over.

When he opened his eyes, it was to the sound of a loud

crash and a yelp. Travis was lying flat on his back with his head half stuck in Sam's toppled trash can.

"Tr ... Travis ..." Demetrius stammered, shaking his head slowly. He seemed shocked to see the boy sprawled out on the floor like that. The emerald glow from Hollister made Travis's face look like he was about to puke.

"I'm good, I'm ... okay," Travis groaned, as he tried to stand up. "No problem here." But he wasn't fooling anyone, especially not Demetrius, who helped Travis to his feet. When Travis could finally stand on his own, he found Demetrius staring at him like he was one fry short of a happy meal.

"What?" Travis shrugged.

Demetrius frowned at Sam, hoping for some explanation for his friend's strange behavior, but Sam had nothing and shrugged. He walked over to his closet, reached in and found his backpack from school. When he turned back around he found Travis staring up at Demetrius, who was scowling and sniffing the air.

"I smell ... pine and," he took in another deep breath, "juniper, I think."

For a minute Sam had no idea what on Earth Demetrius was talking about but then he smelled it too and suddenly it all came back to him.

"Oh, yeah, that's called Mountain Mist," he said.

"Mountain Mist," Demetrius repeated, nodding in approval. "I like it."

"Yeah, not bad," Sam replied. "It smells better than it did before, take my word for it."

"Yeah, take his word for it," Travis said, nodding in agreement. He picked up a book that was lying on top of

Sam's dresser and started flipping through it.

Demetrius gazed at Sam's dragon posters. He looked carefully, taking in every variety of dragon that Sam had displayed on his wall.

"Impressive collection," he said.

Sam stuffed in a few shirts and a hoodie into his backpack and looked up at Demetrius.

"Yeah, I like them. My dad was a big fan of them too, or at least that's what my mother said." Demetrius glanced at Sam from the corner of his eye when he mentioned his father, but Sam turned to admire his collection.

It bothered him that he didn't know that little fact about his father firsthand and he tried to conceal this from Demetrius, but he felt he was doing a poor job. Sam moved to his dresser, putting a few pairs of jeans and some underwear into the backpack.

Demetrius looked back to the wall and trailed his hand softly over one of the posters, as if he was reliving some sort of distant memory. "Yes, Rylan was a big fan of dragons. This was his favorite, you know, the Romanian Diamondback. Rare breed."

Sam looked up at the poster and a smile crept to the corners of his mouth. It felt good to have something in common with his father, even if he never knew him. That one small connection made his father seem real, and that meant more to Sam than anyone could possibly imagine.

Demetrius reached up and removed the poster from the wall and held it out to Sam. Sam reached for the poster but he hesitated, pulling his hand back instead. He searched Demetrius's face, unsure of what to do.

"You should take this," Demetrius said, holding the picture. He stared down at the poster and Sam could not help but notice how sad he looked.

"Life is made of many bonds, not all of which can be seen. This is a bond between you and your father," he said, pursing his lips and handing Sam the picture. "Rylan would have liked that."

Sam felt a sudden warmth radiate throughout his body. He liked that maybe he and his father did have some kind of bond, even if he was no longer alive. He took the poster and placed it neatly into his backpack. Then he turned and grabbed the Christmas picture of Sarah, his mother, and him to put in his bag as well.

He remembered how he had begged his mother to stay home that day, telling her that family Christmas pictures were lame, and that taking them at PhotoSmart inside Wal-Mart was even worse, to which Sarah added that he was already lame and it wouldn't matter. Now, as he looked at his Mom and Sarah in their ridiculous short haircuts it made him smile. He missed them even more now, and he didn't even mind looking at himself in that ridiculous blue and white snowman sweater.

Sam stared at the picture, lost in the details of that day when Travis said, "I guess I should get home and get my stuff too." His words broke Sam's concentration. With everything that had happened, he hadn't given any thought, really, to Travis joining him on his journey to Haven. Or that after tonight Sam might never see him again.

Travis still had family here, not to mention that their journey would be dangerous, so dangerous that they might not survive. As much as Sam wanted Travis to go, there was no way he could ask him to do that for him. What if Travis got injured, or, even worse, if he died? Sam knew he could not live with that. He looked over at Travis, who was thumbing through the pages of the book he'd picked up.

"Is this Pirate book any good? The girl on the cover kind of looks like Sarah."

"Trav, what are you talking about?" Sam asked.

Travis held up the book, waving it in his hand.

"Any good?"

"No, Trav, about going?"

Demetrius watched patiently, glancing back and forth between Sam and Travis. Travis placed the book back on the dresser and looked back at Sam.

"I'm saying I need to get some stuff too, dude. I can't wear these clothes—they have Viper guts on them," he said, looking at Sam as if he were the clueless one.

"But Trav," Sam said with a look of concern, "you can't go."

Travis winced as if the words stung him. "What?" he asked, wiping his hair out of his eyes so he could look at Sam clearly. "What do you mean?"

"Trav, I'm not coming back. I have nothing to come back to," Sam said. "My parents are dead, my sister is dying, and I'm about to take some journey that I might not survive. Besides, you can't leave your grandparents. Who would take care of them?"

Travis jerked his head back slightly, frowned, and moved away from the dresser to stand in front of Sam. "Wait, are you saying that I can't go with you?" Now Demetrius was looking at Travis with his eyebrows raised.

"Um ..." Sam hesitated, "no, I'm saying you *shouldn't* come."

Travis's eyes grew wide. "Shouldn't?"

"Travis, what about you grandparents?" Sam asked, throwing his hands in the air.

Travis's body stiffened; he looked frustrated. "I ... I don't know, I could call my Uncle Keven. He could watch them."

"But Travis," Sam said, shaking his head. "I'm not coming back. You would never see them again."

Travis looked down at his feet, "I know."

Sam moved closer to him. "Do you? Listen to yourself! You are talking about leaving forever. What would you even tell them?"

"I don't know, I don't know!" Travis's voice was louder now. "Something," he said and began pacing around the room.

"Something," Sam said. "Come on, Travis, are you really going to leave your family?"

Travis turned and rounded on Sam. "You're my family too!" he shouted. His face was red and screwed up with anger. "Don't you get it?" He waved his hand in frustration. "You guys have been the family I never had. Geez, Sam, I thought you understood that."

Sam felt like he had been punched in the chest. Travis never raised his voice. He had always been so passive, but now he was really angry.

"Travis ... I—"

"Sam, you can't ask me to turn my back on my family. I won't do it. I won't," he said adamantly. "Yes, my grandparents need me, but so do you. You might think you don't, but you do! I know the risk and it's my choice. Don't take that from me, Sam, please."

"But Trav ..."

"I could never live with myself if I stayed behind. I couldn't live knowing you and Sarah were in danger and I stayed here and did nothing." Travis took a step toward Sam with a look of desperation on his face. "So, I'm asking you again, please. Don't take that choice from me."

There was a long pause while Sam and Travis stared at one another. Demetrius stood quietly with both hands on his staff. He looked back and forth between the two boys until Sam finally spoke. "Okay."

Travis let out a long sigh and placed a hand on Sam's shoulder. "Okay."

CHAPTER 21

"Travis," Demetrius said as he walked toward him, "I think I can help you with your grandparents."

Travis and Sam both turned to face him. "Really? How?" Travis asked, his tone full of skepticism.

"I can help them to forget," Demetrius said calmly. Travis narrowed his eyes.

"What do you mean ... forget?"

Demetrius rubbed his hand along the side of his thin, gray beard and looked up to the ceiling as if he was working out the finer details of a grand plan.

"Yes ... Coppertop I think."

Travis's eyes grew wide. "Um, no offense, Demetrius, but that guy's from the shallow end of the gene pool. I don't want Mr. Happy anywhere near my grandparents."

Sam could tell by Demetrius's raised eyebrow that he was not entirely sure what Travis had just said. But he understood that Coppertop would be a problem.

"No, we don't need Coppertop to meet your grandparents. That would probably be a bad idea. But we do need what Coppertop has on him," Demetrius said.

"And what's that?" Sam asked.

"Silver Ever-lace," he said with a gleam in his eye.

Demetrius turned to the Centurion outside Sam's bedroom door. "Lucio, find Coppertop. I need a flask of Silver Ever-lace."

"Yes, sir." The Centurion nodded, then turned and evaporated.

While they waited for Lucio to return, Sam looked around the room one last time. He had packed most of what he thought he would need for the journey, which wasn't much because his backpack was rather small.

"Demetrius, what about the rest of the stuff in the house, like my mom's and Sarah's things?" he asked as he looked around the room. His gaze fell on his Sony PlayStation.

"Coppertop will take care of all that, so don't worry. It will all be coming with us." Demetrius reassured him.

Travis noticed Sam's gaze, walked over, and placed his hand on the PlayStation. "Yeah, I'm gonna miss my old Jessy. She was good to me."

Sam smirked. "Jessy? You named your PlayStation Jessy?"

Travis frowned and looked offended. "Whatever, Sam, you were never a serious gamer like me. Think of it like a racecar driver referring to his car with a pet name."

"Yeah, I get the symbolism, Speed Racer," Sam smirked.

"Whatever."

"So, why Jessy?"

Travis began to blush. "Oh, well, long story."

Sam raised an eyebrow. "Why Jessy?" he asked again, his gaze turning into a hard stare. Travis grimaced and sighed.

"Fine! You want to break a man down? I named it after ... Jessica Rabbit. There, you happy?"

Sam could not help but laugh. The feeling almost felt foreign to him now. "Wha ... What? Why Jessica Rabbit?"

"I was like five, dude, I don't know!" Travis said, throwing his hands up in the air.

Sam shook his head, grinning. "Yeah, well, I've got a pretty good idea why."

"Yeah, yeah ... get your mind out of the gutter, perv!" Travis groaned and plopped himself on Sam's bed.

Sam smiled as he surveyed the room for anything else he might need, when suddenly the room was illuminated with a flash of blue light and Lucio emerged, holding a silver flask in his armored glove.

"The flask, sir," he said, holding out a small bottle. "Coppertop wasn't particularly happy about relinquishing the potion but Mahan persuaded him."

Demetrius took the flask from the Centurion. "Thank you, Lucio."

"Yes, sir," The soldier replied.

Demetrius turned to Sam and Travis. "This should solve your problem," he said, and held up the silver flask. A series of black ligatures separated by small symbols lined the top and bottom of the container.

Travis stood up from the bed. "What does it do?"

Demetrius unscrewed the top of the flask and poured a few drops of the thick liquid into the cap. The opalescent potion sparkled and swirled on its own, emitting a perfumed smell into the air. Sam thought it was alive at first, like a large microorganism. But it wasn't, he finally concluded, it just looked bizarre, like everything else from this other world.

"Silver Ever-lace is a very powerful potion," Demetrius said. "It has the ability to erase the memory of those who drink it. With the proper incantation it can be directed to erase a specific situation, place, or thing, even a person's entire memory. Not only will it wipe the memory of the one who drinks it, but any they come in contact with as well. It will continue to spread like this until the memory and everything related to it becomes nonexistent.

"So, like, if my grandmother takes it and then talks to my grandfather about me, they'll both forget me?" Travis asked.

"Correct, "Demetrius said, "like you never existed. But you can also protect certain people from memory loss if you wish. Again, it all boils down to the proper incantation."

"So, I'm guessing you have used this before and you know the incantation?" Sam asked.

"Yes," Demetrius replied. "I have had to use it once or twice, depending on the mission I was on. But there was no time for me to acquire the potion before coming here since it's a controlled substance. Proper procedures must be followed. Coppertop, on the other hand, being from the Department of Magical Sterilization, carries it with him at all times."

"Great, a guy like that can wipe memories ... I could have lived without knowing that," Travis said shaking his head.

"Well, it's regulated with a memory charm." Both Sam and Travis looked puzzled. "Meaning that every time the potion is used the bottle will record how it was used and by whom. Flasks of Silver Ever-lace are always turned in to the Magical Artifacts Department for analysis after a mission is complete."

Sam nodded like he understood everything Demetrius said, and it seemed to be enough for Travis too. "Okay so ... what do we do now?" Travis asked.

"Wait, Trav," Sam said as he took a step closer to Travis. "This is big. I mean, are you really okay with this? There is no going back. After tonight your grandparents will never know you even existed."

Travis stared at Sam with a probing gaze, then lifted his chin, cleared his throat, and his expression became serious.

"The way I see it, Sam, is that I have two choices. Stay with my grandparents who may live another five years if I'm lucky or say goodbye now, on my own terms. I choose ... my own terms," he said with a sense of finality in his tone. "I hate having to choose, but I know I can't stand by and do nothing and have the only other people I consider family walk out of my life." Travis paused and looked down to the floor. "I can't do it, Sam. I just can't do it." He took in a deep breath before looking back up. "They have my uncle Keven so I know they will be taken care of. Besides, you need me, Sam. You might not think you do, but you do. You need your family."

Sam thought for a moment before speaking. He wondered what he would do if the tables were turned. Could he leave his grandparents if he had any? Could he risk his life to help someone he thought of as family? The answer to that question, he realized, was yes, he could. He was doing that already for Sarah and he would do it for anyone he considered family.

"Okay, Trav," Sam said and pursed his lips. "I understand."

Travis smiled and sighed in relief. "'Bout time," he said and turned to look back at Demetrius, "So, you were saying?"

Demetrius raised his eyebrows. He seemed caught off guard, as if he wasn't sure Sam and Travis were really done talking. After a moment's pause he said, "I will take you to your home, Travis, where we can administer the potion. Sam will remain behind with Mahan. Demetrius looked to Sam. "Are you okay with that?"

"Um, yeah, I guess, but why can't I go with you?" Sam asked.

"I think the fewer people that go the better. I don't exactly blend in and the three of us together might draw unwanted attention. Besides, you will be safer here."

Sam didn't necessarily like that answer but said nothing more about it.

"Lucio, please take Sam here down below with Mahan."

The large Centurion turned and moved into the room, his magnificent armor reflecting the green and blue light that illuminated from the gemstones of the staffs.

"Yes, sir," he replied.

Demetrius poured the contents of the Silver Ever-lace back into the flask and stowed it beneath the chest plate of his armor. He then took a step forward and brought Hollister between Travis and himself. "It's time, Travis."

Travis looked at Hollister and his face sank. "Yeah, okay," he sighed as he placed a hand around the staff. Sam thought he already looked squeamish; he knew he wasn't looking forward to evaporating again.

There was a green flash and the two bodies disappeared, leaving behind the familiar green mist in their wake. Sam zipped his backpack up, threw it over his shoulder, and took one final look around his room. He would miss this place. After all, it had been his room for thirteen years.

Sam looked up at Lucio and gave a tight smile. "I guess I'm ready, Lucio." The Centurion nodded and placed his elegant silver staff between them. Sam took in a deep breath, knowing what came next. Slowly he placed his hand on the staff and hooked his thumb through the strap of his backpack. The shaft was warm, the room was silent, and then everything went dark.

When Sam reappeared he was standing on the bottom floor near the front door, and for the first time he didn't feel like he wanted to throw up after evaporating. He glanced over at Lucio, who was looking down at him. Sam could see his blue eyes through the dark recesses of his helmet.

"Thanks for the ride," he said. Lucio nodded and then evaporated, returning to his post upstairs.

Sam walked toward Mahan, who was standing guard near the back of the living room watching Coppertop. Two long, slender cases, his mother's Quarrem, and Poppy lay at Coppertop's feet. Sam assumed the slender cases were the Viper's sword and Nara. Moving next to Mahan, Sam watched as Coppertop, with his wild hair and wiry body, began waving his wand in a large circular motion, turning clockwise each time his hand completed a full circle. Sam heard him repeating the same phrase over and over.

"Clean thy air and all that be. Leave nothing behind for man to see."

Golden sparks shot from the tip of his wand and moved through the air, as if they were riding a gentle breeze around the room. Sam stood captivated as the shimmering sparks moved faster and faster until they were swirling like a giant dust storm in the center of the living room. The velocity of currents rattled the walls as pieces of broken furniture and debris rose from the floor, consumed by the swirling winds. Piece by piece, the wreckage was swept into the vortex and disappeared into the golden blur.

Sam could feel his hair whipping around his face. He was scared that something was going to fly out of the vortex and crush them.

"Is this supposed to be happening?" he yelled over the whistling winds to Mahan. But before Mahan could reply everything suddenly stopped and floated in midair—all except for the golden sparkles, which fell ever so lightly, like dust to the ground and vanished.

Coppertop looked over at Sam, and smiled, revealing his stained, yellow teeth again. Then he waved his wand in a circle like a mad conductor.

Sam watched as the smallest splinters and the largest pieces of wood flew together to form furniture again. Loose wires were sucked back into the walls, stagnant water from burst pipes disappeared, leaving the ground dry. The once demolished kitchen looked spotless with gleaming countertops and sparkling faucets. He watched in astonishment as the staircase and the top landing repaired itself and the banister flew back, landing slowly on top of its spindles.

Sam couldn't believe his eyes; within a matter of minutes the entire house was back to normal. *This is magic I could get into,* he thought. Cleaning his room and the garage would be a piece of cake if he knew how to do all that.

"Wow, that was amazing!" he said, still looking around the room in disbelief. Coppertop looked over at Sam, quite proud of himself.

"There aren't none better, boy!" he said grinning. Sam walked around the room, captivated at what he saw. There was not a single thing damaged, scratched, or out of place now. The house was just as it had been before the chaos, before the Vipers. But his walk slowed when he reached the coffee table and saw his mother's mug of green tea and her copy of *Stretching A Dollar* by Reginald Blum. He felt a tightness in his throat and then looked away and stared down at his feet.

He wished he could go back and change what happened but he knew that was impossible, and letting his head fill with self-loathing thoughts was not helping anyone. He needed to be stronger, he told himself. He needed to keep his emotions locked down and focus on what lay ahead.

Sam turned to adjust his backpack on his shoulder when a burst of green light erupted in the center of the room. The next thing he saw was Demetrius grabbing Travis before he hit the ground.

"It's okay, I have you!" Demetrius said.

Sam walked to the center of the room. Travis looked pale and his skin was a little blotchy.

"You okay, Trav?" Sam asked.

"Well, I'm not sure," he groaned, "but if the power is back on and your house has magically put itself back together, then yeah."

Sam smiled, "Then you're okay."

Travis's eyes scanned room. "So, how did this happen?"

Sam tilted his head in Coppertop's direction. "He did it. It was pretty awesome."

"Man, this place looks better than before," Travis said, looking around.

"Yeah, I know," Sam agreed.

Demetrius helped Travis to stand up straight, which wasn't easy considering the large camping backpack he had strapped to his shoulders.

"Wow, did you pack your whole closet, Trav?" Sam asked.

"Yeah, I got a little carried away," Travis said. Sam noticed he had changed clothes too. He was wearing a ridiculous *Star Wars* t-shirt, jeans, and sneakers.

"Seriously, Trav, where did you get that shirt?"

Travis looked down at his t-shirt, which had a picture of Darth Vader's head on it and a caption that read, *Sith Happens*. "What?" he said. "I love this shirt! My uncle Keven gave it to me and I never get to wear it."

Sam shook his head, "I can't believe you chose that shirt to go to another world in."

"Whatever, it's not like they'll even get it. Right, Demetrius?" Demetrius was staring down at his t-shirt.

"What's a Sith?" he asked.

"You see?" Travis said, happy to prove his point. Sam just shook his head again. It was funny, though, just to hear Demetrius say the word Sith.

"All done here, Lore!" a voice called out behind them. It was Coppertop. He was leaning against the kitchen counter petting Poppy, who was sprawled out on the bar above the sink.

"The only thing left is the sweep up. But I need you to leave for that," he grunted.

Sam and Travis looked over to Demetrius.

"Sweep up?" Sam asked.

Demetrius nodded. "He will clear the house of all your belongings, which will be sent to the Majesty for storage until you are ready for them. Then he can cast an autosensory charm on the house."

"What does that do?" Travis asked.

"It will give the illusion to anyone who is looking at the house that someone still lives here. From time to time they will even think they see you and your family coming and going."

"Wow," Travis said, looking over at Coppertop. Coppertop sneered.

"I'm good, boy."

"Yes, quite impressive, Coppertop," Demetrius added glumly.

"The best!" Coppertop continued. "There aren't none better. You won't find a trace of dark magic in the human bunghole!"

"Yes, and always pleasant," Demetrius whispered. "I am sure we won't," he said louder with a pained smile. "We'll let you get back to it. I know you still have perimeter work to do." Coppertop squinted, loathing Demetrius's very existence.

"Well, of course I do. There is always perimeter work to be done." He spun around and walked to the kitchen door. "Poppy, come!" he yelled.

The black cat sprung from the kitchen counter onto the floor and dashed out the door behind Coppertop.

"You know," Travis said, shaking his head and frowning as he stared at the back door, "there are kids that ride the short bus and then there are kids that lick the windows on the short bus. Guess which one he was?"

Sam laughed. "Hey, how did it go with your grandparents?" he asked.

"Well, just like Demetrius said, a couple of drops of the Silver stuff and they were wondering who I was. But thank God we did that after I packed. My whole room disappeared!"

"What?" Sam asked.

"Yeah, Demetrius performed the incantation and everything that remotely had anything to do with me just up and vanished. Demetrius said it would wipe everything, including my crappy grades at school! Anything and everything related to me. Like I never existed."

"So," Sam hesitated, "you're okay? I'm mean, with leaving them and all?"

"I love them and I'll miss them, but they'll be in good hands with my Uncle Keven. I called him before we got started and told him there was a problem with our refrigerator so he's on his way. I think once he gets there and gets his mind erased, he'll be all about watching over them," Travis said.

Sam looked at Travis and smiled. "I'm glad you're coming Trav. Means a lot."

Travis smiled and shook it off. "Well, every Han needs a Chewy."

Sam grinned, "I guess."

"You know which one you are, right?" Travis said laughing.

"Well, boys, it's time," Demetrius said. Their smiles faded and they turned to Demetrius, who had both hands on Hollister again. "It's time to go."

CHAPTER 22

Sam stepped out the back door into the warm, humid night. The smell of large oak trees filled the air as they swayed back and forth in the night breeze. Barron was crouched down by the garage, pawing at a water bug without a care in the world, never knowing what had happened in the house that night. In fact no one on Earth would know the tragic loss Sam had suffered at the hands of the mystical creature they called the Viper. Humans didn't know about things like that, and it was better that way.

The world, *this* world, was not ready for that kind of knowledge. Humans lived in a world of expectance and comprehension. They needed to be able to understand a thing like magic for it to become a normality in their lives.

But Sam didn't think they would ever understand the supernatural. He wasn't even sure if he did, and he had an advantage most humans didn't. His parents were supernatural, and he probably was too.

As he stood in the summer breeze he felt different than he had before. He felt as if he could touch and feel everything miles away from him. Like he was part of something much bigger than the here and now. He could smell the Earth around him as he never could before. It was richer, stronger, but calming at the same time. Then there was the water—he couldn't see it, but he could feel it somehow. He was aware of its presence beneath the surface. It felt like it was pulling him, wanting to connect. He didn't know exactly what that meant. But something was different; something had changed within him and he was scared to think what that might be.

Sam took one last look at his home and for the first time he saw the house for what it was—memories. Memories he would cherish for the rest of his life, memories of a time that was simple, yet precious. A time that he had taken for granted because he'd thought it would last forever.

But he had been a fool, he told himself, because nothing lasted forever. The twisting knots in Sam's stomach were more than sorrow or regret—he was nervous too. He was about to leave the place he had lived his entire life. He wasn't simply moving to another state or something trivial like that. He was about to leave his *planet* and that was worth getting a little nervous about.

The silver moonlight cast half-shadows on Travis with his large black backpack strapped to his shoulders. He stood silently facing the wind as it blew softly though his light brown hair, his eyes gazing up at the stars, as if it was the last time he would ever see them.

Demetrius was the last to walk through the back door with his long black staff in hand and the hood of his cloak pulled tightly over his head. As he approached, his eyes cut to Coppertop in the corner of the yard, waving his wand

and muttering his spells. For an instant, Sam thought he did look like Dirty Ernie pillaging around through the trash.

"Demetrius," Sam said, still watching Coppertop perform his magic. There was a slight hesitation in his voice but he continued, "is your magic the same as Coppertop's?"

Demetrius looked down at Sam, his pursed lips forming a smile. "No, Keepers do not have that ability to conjure magic. We use Callings."

"What are callings?" Travis asked, looking at Demetrius now.

"Well ... Callings look similar to magic to the untrained eye," Demetrius said, "but they are very different. You see, magic comes from within and it is rare for humans to possess it. A Calling, however, is nature's magic in its purest form. To perform a Calling is to summon the very essence of nature. The ability to Call a specific element like Earth, Air, or Water and wield it can be difficult. It is very powerful and that's where a good staff comes in handy," he said, lifting Hollister in his hand.

"What's so important about the staff? I mean, how does it help?" Sam asked, wrinkling his brow. He wanted to know as much as he could about magic and Callings so he could try and understand what he was up against.

"The staff is used as a conductor," Demetrius continued. "It helps to regulate and control the Calling so it can be channeled properly. Each staff is unique to its user and is made with any number of properties and combinations that contribute to the overall delivery and effectiveness for the Calling."

Sam and Travis stood in silence, their minds trying to grasp what Demetrius had just said. The thought of magic and Callings was all so absurd a few days ago. But now it was as real as the air they breathed.

"What about Fire? You didn't mention Fire," Travis said. Demetrius turned, his eyebrows furrowed with concern.

"Fire is the deadliest of all the elements to control. Even the most experienced Elementalist, such as myself, does not dare use it. There have been many in the past who have tried and few have lived to tell the tale. In the beginning, an Elementalist is pulled toward the element they have the strongest affinity for. You can tell which element this is by the color of their gemstone on their staff."

Sam and Travis looked at Hollister's emerald gemstone, "Earth," Sam said pointing to the stone.

"Yes, and your mother's was Water. That is why—"

"Sapphire," Sam blurted. "That's why Nara's gemstone is a blue sapphire."

"That is correct," Demetrius said.

Sam stood for a moment, taking in what Demetrius had said. He knew going forward that both Travis and he were more of a liability than an asset. They didn't know magic or how to Call an element. The floating baseball could have been an accident, something to do more with the spell than with himself. Demetrius would have to protect them, like he had earlier, until they could learn to defend themselves.

Sam looked at Demetrius again, who was now gazing up at the stars. Demetrius closed his eyes and breathed in slowly. He exhaled and smiled, almost as if he were acknowledging something no one else could hear.

"Right then," he said, looking down at the boys, "time to go. Are you ready?"

Sam looked over at Travis, who gave a halfhearted smile and nodded his head in agreement.

"We're ready," Sam said, trying to sound as confident as possible.

"Very well then," Demetrius replied. "Now, we must travel back to the portal just beyond your village. From there we will pass through the gateway and into Haven. Any questions?" he asked, as if surely they had none.

Sam and Travis looked at one another hesitantly. Sam raised his eyebrow and Travis shrugged his shoulders. Then together they turned to Demetrius and replied, "No."

"Very well," Demetrius said as he positioned his staff between the two of them. Sam and Travis placed their hands on the shaft and Demetrius tapped the ground once. Everything went dark and Sam felt his stomach drop and then, in what felt like an instant, he heard a loud splash.

"Hollister, light," Demetrius said and his staff became brighter, illuminating the cave around them. Travis was lying face down in the shallow water scrambling to get to his feet.

"Travis!" Sam yelled stepping in front of Demetrius to reach him. "Geez!"

The water was ice cold as Travis sloshed around frantically, trying to regain his footing.

"I'm okay," he grunted.

"Are you sure?" Demetrius asked. His eyes illuminated like glass in the green glow.

"Yeah, yeah I'm fine." Travis said, clearly frustrated with himself.

When Sam and Travis were finally able to look at their

surroundings they noticed the familiar glittering cavern walls and massive stalactites hanging from the ceilings.

"You have got to be kidding me!" Travis said as he looked cautiously around the cave. "There are spiders here you know, big ones!"

"Demetrius," Sam said, "we've been here before. This is where we first saw the spiders—or the Vipers, as it turned out!"

"Are there spiders here now?" Travis asked, shivering.

"No," Demetrius replied, "just this." He pointed Hollister to the large, gold and silver floating mirror.

"The mirror," Sam gasped.

"That's where the spiders came from last time!" Travis explained.

"Yes, it's the portal," Demetrius said.

Suddenly, shrieking sounds echoed from above them as several bats flew by in the darkness.

"Oh, and there's bats too, lots of them!" Travis added.

Demetrius turned toward the mirror. "Come, this way." He moved forward with his staff held high and wadded through the water with Sam and Travis close behind.

The golden mirror glimmered in the dark as Demetrius's staff flickered in its reflection. Gold and silver inlays shined as his staff moved toward one of the surrounding Zodiac symbols. Demetrius lifted his staff and gently tapped several symbols with its end, illuminating each one with a white-blue glow. The mirror came to life with a resonating hum. Demetrius removed one black triangular crystal from within his cloak and slid it into the bottom of the mirror next to another already in the frame. The crystals resembled the ones Sam had seen in his mother's Quarrem.

Just like before, the large mirror hummed louder and squeals from above rang out as hundreds of bats took flight. Each of the Zodiac signs shined bright gold except for the ones that Demetrius had touched. Demetrius removed the onyx crystals from their sheath in the mirror just beneath the Water symbol and stowed them in his cloak before taking a step back.

"Oh, here we go again!" Travis said, just loud enough to be heard over the mirror's hum.

Their reflections began to quiver as if they were looking into a small pond. The large, gold frame descended slowly and the humming became louder, producing small vibrations in the shallow water that exposed the cavern floor beneath it. The mirror continued to drop until it was resting on the bottom of the shallow pool.

"I shall enter first to make sure the way is safe," Demetrius said loudly. "Then you must follow one at a time. Do you understand?" He had to yell over the loud humming.

The two boys looked at one another and Travis nodded.

"Yes, we understand!" Sam yelled back.

He watched intently as Demetrius lowered his head and moved forward into the massive, golden mirror. His body entered slowly, as if he were walking through water, and the silver mirror rippled as it engulfed his body. Then Sam saw the same image he had seen before—moonlight and the tall trees of the forest.

"It looks like we're headed for more water!" Travis yelled.

"What?" Sam said. "Water, where?"

Travis pointed to the mirror. "There, don't you see it? Through the mirror!"

But Sam didn't see water, he saw a forest. "No, I see trees, and lots of them."

"What?" Travis said, putting his hand to his ear. The humming was so loud now Sam could barely hear himself speak.

Sam turned to Travis and yelled, "I. See. Trees!"

"Trees? I don't see any trees! Travis replied.

Maybe that's how it worked—maybe they saw what they wanted to see, Sam thought. Surely if something could go wrong Demetrius would have warned them about it. Travis saw more water and Sam saw a forest like he had seen ... in his dream.

He felt a terrifying wave of realization sweep over him. He looked back to the mirror and gasped.

"Sarah."

The memory of the dream came rushing back. He could see the forest, the moonlight, the beast chasing him, and Sarah calling his name. He had not put the two together before, but now it was all too clear. That was the same forest. He looked at Travis, unsure of what to say or how to explain it.

Travis looked at Sam, his eyes trying to meet Sam's as he placed his hand on his shoulder.

"Buddy, you okay?" he yelled. He gave him a gentle shake. "You don't look good."

Sam broke from his reverie, pursed his lips, and nodded that he was fine. He wasn't sure what it was that he was seeing but he knew one thing—he wasn't going to find the answers on this side of the mirror. It was time to go.

"Ok, your turn. I'll take up the rear," Sam said as loudly as he could.

"No, Sam you go!" Travis replied. "I got this!"

"I'll be fine. I'll be right behind you," Sam said, patting him on the back.

The boys looked at one another as the sound of the humming of the mirror flooded their senses. Travis gave Sam one final grin and a thumbs-up before turning and walking, head down, into the mirror. With a small ripple, Travis was gone and Sam was left standing all alone. He edged closer to the mirror and apprehensively placed a single finger into the rippling forest. To his surprise, it was cool to the touch and not wet like he had expected. The ripples moved from around his finger out in small circles that expanded to the edges of the frame. Sam pulled his finger back and stared into the moonlit forest.

"I can do this," he said to himself. He swallowed hard and hitched up his backpack. Then he lowered his head and stepped forward into the world called Haven.

About the Author

D.C. Akers was born in Texas and attended Crowley High School. After spending several years working in accounting, Akers began to pursue his childhood dream of becoming a writer.

Like many who enjoy the fantasy genre, Akers started reading it as an adolescent. He was fascinated with Tolkien's *Lord of the Rings* and Bram Stoker's *Dracula*. He currently enjoys reading works by Dean Koontz, Heather Brewer, J.K. Rowling, and Rick Riordan.

BOOK THREE

HAVEN

ELIXIR OF LIFE

Haven: A Stranger Magic Audio book is now available
at Amazon.com, Audible, and iTunes!
Listen to a sample today for free!